PRE Stolen DOLLS

KER DUKEY & K WEBSTER

Pretty Stolen Dolls
Copyright © 2016 Ker Dukey and K Webster

Editing: Word Nerd Editing
Formatting: Champagne Formats
Cover Design: K Webster

ISBN-13: 978-1537462417
ISBN-10: 1537462415

ALL RIGHTS RESERVED. This book contains material protected under International and Federal Copyright Laws and Treaties. Any unauthorized reprint or use of this material is prohibited. No part of this book may be reproduced or transmitted in any form or by any means, electronic or mechanical, including photocopying, recording, or by an information and retrieval system without express written permission from the Author/Publisher.

This is a work of fiction. Names, characters, places, and incidents either are the product of the author's imagination or are used fictitiously, and any resemblance to actual persons, living or dead, business establishments, events, or locales is entirely coincidental.

Note from Ker and K,

Pretty Stolen Dolls has themes that some may find offensive. If you're a sensitive reader please read with caution.

We ask that you please take care when sharing your reviews, and hopefully enthusiasm for this title, to not spoil any parts for others. Thank you for choosing to read this book and we hope you enjoy every chapter.

DEADICATION

For all our stolen, lost, broken, damaged, hurting,
wounded, dirty, and pretty dolls out there.

Miss Dukey had a concept that was sick, sick, sick.
So she called K. Webster to come quick, quick, quick.
Webster came with her smirk and evil mind,
And she said, let's give them a book that is one of a kind.
So they teamed up together with plots, plots, plots.
With darkness and passion there would be lots, lots, lots.
As they wrote, sinful, dark, and some filthy muck,
They agreed their readers would call them
twisted as fuck.

We love you guys.

"It is an anxious, sometimes a dangerous thing to be a doll. Dolls cannot choose; they can only be chosen; they cannot 'do'; they can only be done by."
−Rumer Godden, The Dolls' House

PROLOGUE

Jade
Eighteen years old...

Daddy always told us to be careful. Not to talk to strangers, no matter how friendly they appeared. To question everyone. With two naïve little girls growing up in a wicked world, he wanted to educate us and explain the evil that ran rampant on the news channels. He forced us to watch the happenings of the world far from what seemed like our own, educating us on the beasts walking the earth with faces just like ours, just like his—even in middle America. We lived on a quiet street in a quiet neighborhood in a quiet town, but that didn't mean the monsters of the world weren't always lurking.

They're everywhere, he said, *not just in the shadows.*

He wanted us to perceive the world with narrowed eyes and closed hearts.

And so I did. I'm my daddy's girl, through and through—a skeptic by nature. Suspicious. Standoffish. Untrusting. I heeded his instructions to the letter and kept my sister and I both safe.

Until I didn't.

Until the day my world spun, turned on its axis, and everything was stolen from *us*.

Or should I say, until *we* were stolen from the world.

Four years ago, I let my guard down for one man. I allowed the curious girl within me to forget the most important message our dad taught us: *not all monsters hunt in the dark*. Dropping my constant guard for the attention of soft, golden brown eyes and a crooked smile, the walls I held strong, weakened, stealing my equilibrium and sending my hormones into chaos. At fourteen years old, I was weak in the knees for a man much older than me.

Benny.

At least, that's the name he told me. He lied about that...*he lied about everything.*

Benny's Pretty Dolls.

I relive that day over and over, fantasizing a different outcome, but I always end up here. My heart still stammers at the memory of first seeing him. I'll never forget that day.

My feet are sore. I should have worn my other sandals like Macy. She skips ahead through the narrow, crowded aisles of the flea market, stopping to gush over anything remotely shiny along the way. How she can be so energetic in this heat astounds me, but that's our Macy—full of life and openly sharing it with the world. Sweat trickles down over my lip and the burst of salt stirs over my tongue, reminding me how thirsty I am. My dress sticks to my damp flesh like an extra layer of skin. It's somehow hotter under the shelter of the tents versus the blazing, unforgiving sun. I swipe away the sweat on my upper lip with the back of my hand and send a nasty glare to one of the grown men with an overhanging tummy, flicking his hungry gaze over my younger

sister while licking his fat lips and adjusting his slacks. Pig.

We need to leave.

I'm worried like Daddy taught me. My heart thunders in my chest with the need to drag my sister back home where Momma is expecting us for supper in the next half hour.

Of course, Macy won't be deterred easily.

Always curious, smiling, and eager to know the world.

The flea market is the highlight of her week and the only freedom outside the perimeters of our street Daddy allows us to have. Every Saturday, she clutches the dollar she earned from helping with random chores around the house and pines over the items she can't afford before settling on a simple toy within her price range, which she will later break or lose and I will have to replace with something of my own to stop the tears she will shed.

As for me, I'm the saver.

Each and every dollar.

Just like Daddy taught me.

One day, I want to go to one of those big cities we always see on the TV shows Momma watches and find those lurking monsters. I'm going to be a policewoman and protect more than just my sister.

I'm not impulsive or rash.

I can wait.

Unfortunately, my sister can't.

"Oh my goodness, Jade," *she says with a squeal, sending a bright smile in my direction, which reflexes my own at her excitement.* "Look how beautiful they are."

I bare my teeth at the man with the potbelly and salacious grin who happened to be walking in the same direction as us for the last ten minutes. He watches my sister as she bends over to pick up a doll from the table. When he notices my death glare, he has the sense to look ashamed and turns away.

"Twenty-eight dollars," she murmurs, a twinge of sadness in her voice.

Jerking my attention to my sister, I smile when I see the doll. It's a twelve-inch porcelain doll with silky chin-length hair and wide hazel eyes—an exact replica of Macy.

"Oh," I gush, "she's beautiful, but too expensive. Pick something else, Macy."

Macy frowns and nods before setting the doll back down on the table. We're just about to walk away when a voice halts us.

"Pretty doll for a pretty doll," a man states in a smooth tone.

Macy and I lift our gazes to the booth owner. The dolls are a thing of the past as we both drink in the handsome guy regarding us with a mischievous crooked grin. A mop of overgrown brown curls hangs down over his eyebrows into his amber-colored eyes. With just the smallest dusting of facial hair, I can tell he's older—maybe early twenties—but he carries an innocence about him that makes him appear younger.

"She can't afford the doll," I tell him, a slight quiver in my voice. He's cute like the guys from the teen magazines Momma sometimes lets us buy from the grocery store when funds aren't too tight.

His gaze darts between us and he grins. "Maybe we can strike a deal. I don't think I quite like it when girls as pretty as you two are sad. I prefer them..." he pauses, his top teeth piercing into his thick bottom lip as he gazes at me in thought. I hold my breath, almost hypnotized as I await his answer. "Smiling." He grins and motions toward me. "How much you got?"

I try not to focus on the fact that he has muscles, unlike Bo from next door. He's a senior in high school and still doesn't have muscles—not like this. This guy is better than Bo, better than those guys in the magazine. He's dreamy. My stomach clenches into knots.

Momma calls these knots hormones. Says I'll be a woman soon. Ack.

"I have a dollar," Macy tells him proudly, lifting her chin, gaining his attention back, and I mourn the loss of it. Her cheeks turn rosy and I suspect she's just as embarrassed to have this cute guy's attention. I want it back on me...

At this, he chuckles. It doesn't seem rude or like he's making fun of her, more like he's entertained by her words— like he thinks she's cute, too.

A pang of jealousy spikes through me. I quickly squash it down and remember I'm supposed to be looking after my sister—protecting her from leering men and getting into trouble. The air begins to feel a little cooler and the crowd starts to thin, alerting me to how much time has passed.

"Come on, Macy," I hiss, snatching her elbow. "We need to get home. These dolls are too expensive. And you know Daddy doesn't want us talking to strangers."

"Benny." He smirks at me. One dark eyebrow disappears under his curls and a small dimple forms in one cheek. "I'm strange, but I'm not a stranger. My name's Benny."

My cheeks heat and I swallow. "We can't afford the doll."

He shrugs, his eyes moving like he's watching a ping

pong match between my sister and I. "Suit yourself." *His shoulders lift in an uncaring shrug and he rearranges the doll so she's back in place.*

Macy swivels around to glare at me. My sister is sweet and carefree; not once have I seen her hazel eyes glimmer with anger. "You have some money saved. Maybe I could borrow a few dollars. I've never had a dolly like this before." *Her eyebrows crash together and her bottom lip protrudes.*

Guilt trickles through me the way the sweat dribbles down my back: slow and torturous.

"I don't have twenty-eight dollars," *I tell him, my voice hoarse.*

His smile is warm and does nothing to cool my heated skin or nerves. Time is ticking and it's a long walk home. "I could sell the doll to you for twenty." *He tilts his head, studying me, and I squirm under his gaze.*

Macy gives me a hopeful look. Her anger is gone and her eyes twinkle with delight.

"Fifteen. All I have is fifteen dollars," *I say in defeat, my breath coming out in a huff.*

Benny scratches at the scruff on his jaw as he contemplates the deal. There's a glimmer of victory on his up-tilted lips. "Fifteen it is."

Letting out a squeal, Macy scoops the porcelain doll into her arm and spins in a circle as she hugs it to her chest. Brat.

"Thank you! I swear I'll pay it back soon!" *she gushes.*

Swallowing, I break the bad news to them both. "The money is at home. I'm not sure I have enough time to get there and back before the flea market closes." *Or if Daddy will allow me to come back once I'm home.*

He frowns, his eyes dragging between us both. "I suppose I can wait."

Macy's hands tremble as she sets the doll back down on the table, clearly defeated.

"Or," he says with an easy grin, "you two could help me pack up here. I'll knock off another five bucks for your services and then I can run you by your house on my way out of here. I can even meet your folks. Who knows, maybe we can talk your dad into buying one for you too." His eyes flit over to mine and my flesh heats again.

"I don't play with dolls anymore," I tell him in a clipped tone. For some reason, I want him to think of me as a girl closer to his age rather than one who plays with dolls like my sister.

Disappointment mars his features and his brows knit together as if I've personally wounded him. I instantly feel horrible and fear he will take back his deal, leaving Macy angry and upset.

"I mean, uh...Daddy doesn't want us taking rides from anyone."

His eyes widen with understanding. "I'm not anyone. I'm Benny."

"Little girl wants a doll?" a deep voice sings behind me. A chill, despite the August heat, creeps up my spine. The scent of alcohol and chewing tobacco suffocates me. "Maybe I should buy one for them both. But what would I get in return?" The man from before has come back, and this time, there's no shame on his face or in his suggestion.

Benny snaps his attention to the man behind me and glares. I'm momentarily stunned by his sudden fierceness and step closer to Macy. "Back the hell away, prick, before I call the police on your pedophile ass."

"Yeah, fuck off, faggot," the man grunts before stomping off.

Moments earlier, I worried Benny was a threat. Now, I realize he's simply a nice guy, wanting a girl to have her doll and warning off predators. Daddy would want to meet the man who scared away a monster.

"Actually," I tell him, my voice brave, "we'll help you. Maybe Daddy will buy me that one." I point to a boy porcelain doll with honey-colored eyes like Benny and messy brown hair.

Benny grins. "You've got yourself a deal, little doll."

"Last box," Benny says with a grunt as he heaves it into the back of his tan, aging van. This must be where all those muscles tensing in his arms came from. These boxes are heavy. Macy and I couldn't even lift one together, but we were good help packing them up.

"Now we can meet your pops and I can try to talk him into two dolls. Does your momma like dolls?"

Macy giggles as he closes the back doors of the van. "She plays Barbie's with me sometimes."

Benny flashes her a smile before opening the side door. It rattles on its hinges. "I like your momma already." His hand motions inside the vehicle.

"I can sit up front," I tell him.

A flicker of emotion passes over his features before he hardens his gaze. "Actually, the hinges on the passenger side door are rusted shut. Damn door might fall off if we open it. You said you live close by. I'll crank up the AC. You'll be fine in the back and we wouldn't want this little doll to be back here on her own." He ruffles Macy's hair and she beams up at him.

I glance nervously at my sister, but she's already climbing into the back of the van.

"I don't know. Maybe we should just call our parents from the payphone. I really don't think Daddy would like us riding with you."

When he starts laughing at me, I turn beet red. "Y-You think I would do something? Like that man earlier? What are you? Twelve?" At this, he snorts. "I'm not into little kids. Trust me."

Anger wells inside me. "I'm fourteen, and I'm not a little kid!" I exclaim, folding my arms in defiance.

"Fourteen?" he whispers, and something akin to disappointment clouds his features. Before I can dwell on the hope he possibly wanted me to be older, he laughs and shrugs.

Maybe I was wrong about the disappointment.

Finally tampering down his laughter, he holds his palms up in defense. "Okay, okay, I get it. You're not a little kid. But little kid or not, I'm not interested in you, short stuff. I typically go for girls with boobs."

Now I'm just annoyed and humiliated. I've been ogling him this entire time and he just sees me as a child. Not that I wanted anything else, but it still pains me a little. With a huff, I climb in to the backseat and cross my arms over my flat chest. "Just take us home."

By the time he climbs in and gets out onto the main road, his humor is gone. He messes with an ice chest in the front seat beside him and retrieves a bottle of water.

"Thirsty?"

God yes.

Macy snatches it out of his hand and greedily gulps down over half the bottle before I steal it from her. The cold moisture seeping down the bottle feels incredible in my hot palm. I polish the rest off within seconds and rub the cold plastic over my neck to steal the remaining frost from the bottle.

"Aren't you going to ask us where we live?" I question after several minutes of driving. He hasn't spoken much at all and that easy smile that once graced his lips is now stoic. His eyes keep tracking me in the overhead mirror. It's hot and stuffy in the back of the van, despite his promise of AC, and I feel lightheaded. My eyes swimming and mind woozy, I reach toward the door handle for stability and grab air... where's the handle? When I glance over at Macy, her head lolls to the side and she curls into the upholstery to get comfortable.

"You already told me," he says, his voice distant.

My eyelids feel heavy and I struggle to keep them open. This heat is really starting to affect me. "I didn't tell you…" Every muscle in my body seems to weaken. My heart thunders in my chest, but I feel powerless to do anything about it. "Take us home," I demand in a slur.

His tone is dark—nothing like the Benny who sweet-talked me into forgetting all our Daddy's lessons. "You will be home."

The world spins around me and a wave of nausea passes over me. "What's wrong with me?" My voice is a mere whisper.

"Nothing. You're perfect. You're both perfect. Exactly what I was looking for. Two precious little dolls."

I barely have the strength to lift the water bottle up. It's then I notice the chalky residue in the bottom of the plastic.

He drugged us. He's a monster—the monster lurking in plain view, just like Daddy warned.

"Help." The soft murmur of my plea can't be heard over Benny's humming. I soon recognize it when he starts singing a nursery rhyme Momma used to sing to us when we were ill.

Miss Polly had a dolly who was sick, sick, sick.

So she phoned for the doctor to be quick, quick, quick.

The doctor came with his bag and hat,
And he knocked at the door with a rat-a-tat-tat.
He looked at the dolly and shook his head,
And he said, "Miss Polly, put her straight to bed!"
He wrote on a paper for a pill, pill, pill,
"I'll be back in the morning, yes I will, will, will."

"Stop," I choke out, but he ignores that I've said anything at all. After he finishes the final verse, he does stop singing, though, and turns on his stereo. Heavy rock music works its way into my head as everything goes blissfully black.

Help.

A soft moan from the cell beside me jerks me back to the present. Bloody dents in my skin from my grip sting as I release the hold I have on my arms. For four years, we've been imprisoned by Benny. *His dolls.* Except I now know his name isn't Benny—or at least, that's not what we're allowed to call him.

Benjamin.

He makes us call him Benjamin.

Benny with the golden brown eyes and easy smile never climbed into the van that day. *There never was a Benny.*

Instead, we willingly got into the vehicle with a monster. A monster who has spent four agonizing years making us his personal dolls, which he likes to play with often—and he's not gentle with his toys.

I'm long past tears; they went with my innocence.

Occasionally, Macy cries when he's being especially brutal, or when he leaves her cell and she pleads with him she can be better. She knows if she doesn't try to be the best dolly she can be, she won't be fed for a day or two.

I'd rather starve than be his good dolly.

Because of this monster and his warped mind, I'm desensitized. Instead of begging and pleading for him to let us go—which always falls on deaf ears and gains us the manic pacing Benjamin, who sings his nursery rhyme and then sits there painting the faces on his dolls—I plot our escape. I plan his death. I make sure to go on breathing so my sister and I have a future.

The wooden door slams shut on the cell beside me with a screech. Whatever he was doing with Macy, he's done now, and her whimpering notches another dent in my heart.

My turn.

I'm always forced to listen to him with her. It's his special way of torture, forcing me to hear her cries so by the time he comes for me, I'm rabid. He loves it when I fight and tear at his flesh any chance I get. The sicko gets off when I go on the offensive. He always takes dresses and makeup into her cell. I hear him decorating her into the perfect doll, but not me. He leaves me bare and untamed.

One of these days, he'll slip up and I'll be ready.

His muscled frame comes into view under the single halogen bulb in front of my cell. He's only wearing a pair of jeans that hang low on his hips. Sweat rolls down his solid chest and his hair is soaked from exertion. Smelling the coppery scent of my little sister's blood on this man is something that will forever be burned into my senses. Erasing that will never be possible unless it's with the scent of his own blood as he gurgles his last breath.

The man who crafts dolls outside our cells on a work station is beyond crazy. He's more monster than man—one more brutal and deranged than Daddy could have ever imagined lurking out there, waiting.

A full-on mentally deranged sicko, and when he wasn't out there working, waiting, taunting, Macy would constantly ask when he was coming back, *if* he was coming back. He always came back and I couldn't save her from it.

When he's in his sick rage, his normally honey-colored eyes darken to more of a milky chocolate. I've watched his every move, listened to his every word, studied his every mannerism.

I know him better than he knows himself.

I know his patterns.

His tells.

His weaknesses.

And one day, I'll pounce. I'll end this and save us—save *her*—like I was supposed to.

"There's my dirty little doll. So wild and scared, but

still so fucking pretty." His eyes narrow as his gaze travels down my body. It's a hundred degrees easily, but I can't help but defy him. I'm not naked and cowering. I've ripped the sheet from the mattress and tied it around my body like a dress. He will take it with him when he leaves and when night falls and the walls to my cell cool, I'll be exposed and wishing for the sheet, but defying him is just too appealing—it's the only ounce of control I possess.

I'm about to smart off to him when I notice the sway. It's slight and almost imperceptible, but I see it. He's drunk. He's *never drunk*. Drunk is good. Drunk means weak.

Fisting my hands at my sides, I wait. An opportunity like this is too big not to act on. When he comes inside, I'll attack him. Surely I can overtake him. There's a swagger to his movements and all I need is for him to let down his guard once.

"Your master wants to play. What game are you going to play with me today, dirty little doll?" he questions, a smile on his lips as he fumbles with the keys.

"We could play Eye Spy, but your dick is so small, no one can really spy it," I snap, goading him.

A low growl rumbles in his throat. "Or I could play with your insides when I gut you for being a bad little dolly."

I was used to his threats. They were always deadly and vicious, but he never followed through with actually killing me. I think he liked my insolence; it made his games more fun for him.

The click of the lock unengaging causes my sweaty skin to erupt with goosebumps. Soon, he'll be inside this cell taking what he wants—just like every night.

Not tonight.

The thought—so sudden and fierce—charges me with adrenaline. And when he drops the keys, the sound chinking around my cell like a starting pistol urging me to go, I make my move. Slinging the door hard to the right, I wrench it open with a rage-filled scream. He barely has a chance to register I've come out of my cell before I slam my fists into his chest and push him hard. His unstable body hits the floor with a *thud*.

"STOP!" he roars as he clambers to his feet.

But I don't stop.

I run for my life. I run for both our lives. If I can get the heck out of this hellhole, I can find help. I can save my sister. I take the stairs, which shockingly lead down two at a time.

His home is a blur as I rush toward a door to the right of a kitchen. I was in an attic turned dolly-dungeon. As if my world weren't screwed up enough, of course it would be straight from a horror movie. I don't stop to inspect the kitchen along the way, to look for a phone, or even look over my shoulder to see if he's coming the moment I shove through the front door.

I.

Don't.

Stop.

Cold air hits me in the face, coating my entire body like a cloak. We're surrounded by woods. Trees, green and vibrant, whizz past as I run as fast as my legs will carry me. I ignore the bite of sticks and pinecones with each step I take. I ignore the scratching of branches as they whip and hiss at my body. Nothing matters but finding help. Behind me, I hear the crunching of leaves and grunting. He's hot on my trail, but not close enough.

He's weak.

Drunk.

An unworthy match.

With each long leap through the thick woods, I distance myself farther from him. Numbing the pain humming throughout my body, I run until my chest aches from my lungs burning for air. I'm dizzy, hungry, and not used to such bursts of exercise, but I don't stop or slow until I'm pretty sure I haven't heard him in ages. Death will take me before I allow him to take me again.

I got away.

I freaking got away. My mind screams at me in hysterics, but no sound leaves my lips.

And I'm going to get her back.

Willing myself to keep going, I take off again, faster this time.

A loud sob escapes as realization courses through me. We're finally free. As soon as I find help, they'll take that psycho to prison and we'll go back home to Momma and Daddy. I'm still holding on to darkened, fading images of my parents in my mind when I bolt from the edge of the woods. A hundred yards ahead is a road. Headlights from about a half-mile away are heading right in my direction. Elation echoes through my bones as I stretch them wide to signal the car coming.

"*Help!*" I screech and power forward.

The vehicle seems to be going slow enough, surely I can wave it down and be rescued.

"*Help!*" My voice is hoarse, but my legs keep moving.

When the vehicle starts to slow, I start crying so hard, I'm blinded. It doesn't stop my journey, though. I run, waving my arms wildly, until my bloody, cut-up feet slap the warm pavement.

"*Help!*"

The screeching of tires signifies the driver saw me. They'll stop for me and save me. They'll help me—

Thud.

Metal slams into me from the side with the force of a speeding train. Bones crack and pop in my body like a symphony of hollow drums. I don't know which way is up until my head slams painfully against the pavement with a crack that resonates inside my skull.

Then, I'm staring up.

Bright stars glitter in the sky as something warm pulsates from the side of my head, soaking the pavement beneath me. I haven't seen the sky in four years. It's bewitching, beautiful, and sparse.

I try to speak when an older woman with greying hair shouts for me to hold on.

But I can't hold on.

The stars dim, the sky darkening and filling the void around me.

Her features fade.

And darkness steals me this time.

Hang in there, Macy. I'm coming back for you.

CHAPTER ONE

Eight years later...

"Jade, is everything okay? You don't look like you're eating."

Lifting my eyes to my mother's worried, searching ones, I smile and spoon in a mouthful of red velvet cake she bought with our coffees. We've made ourselves comfortable in a small diner in town. The bright red leather booth seats are peeling at the seams, but the food is good and the coffee is even better.

"I'm fine, Mom, and weigh more than I ever have."

It was true. I had to use a coat hanger to hook the buttonhole and stretch it to meet the button on my favorite jeans this morning.

"You should come home for a cooked meal. Your father would love to see you." The smile she offers crinkles her eyes.

Picking up the mug of coffee and letting the heat soak into my palms through the cup, I inhale the steam billowing from the top. "I will soon. I promise. Things are just really busy at work."

She stirs a spoon around her cup absentmindedly.

"You worked so hard to make detective and then they threw you straight into the deep end and haven't let you up to take a breath."

It's weird that she still wants to talk about this. She knows how much I wanted this job and how hard I had to work to get it. I missed four years of education being locked away from the world. I had to do night classes, summer school, and study twice as hard as everyone else. "I like working," I tell her, my voice rising a few octaves. "If I don't keep busy, I go back there in my mind and I…"

Her face blanches, just like it does every time I mention what happened. It's been years now, but it's still with me, like a ghost haunting me from the shadows. Mom and Dad don't like to talk about it. They tried to pick up from where we left off when I was a fourteen-year-old girl, naïve and gullible. That girl died in that cell the first time Benny put his hands on her.

The scent of flowers invades me when a woman and child walk past. She's wearing too much perfume and her blue eyeshadow matches the overstuffed bright blue bag she's carrying. An item drops from it and hits the floor, rolling to my foot. Bending down, I reach for it and pause. It's a doll. Just a simple dolly, but it causes all the hairs on my body to rise and my mind to race into overdrive.

Was it a sign?

Is he back?

Did he tell them to drop it?

Is he in here, watching me?

I pick the doll up from the floor and call out to the woman, "Excuse me." I stand and walk the six or seven feet to the front of the diner. "You dropped this."

The woman's eyes grow wide and her mouth pops open. "Oh my God, thank you. She won't sleep without it." She sighs, taking the doll and stuffing it deeper into her bag this time. I wiggle my fingers down at the little girl, whose wide blue eyes hypnotize me. She huddles into her mother's thigh and smiles up at me.

"Jade," Mom calls when I'm still standing there, my hands tucked in the back pockets of my jeans, staring at the door the woman and child exited through a good twenty seconds ago.

I hate taking time off—too much time to think and dwell and remember. It was rare for me to actually take a day, but I promised Mom I'd meet her for coffee and shopping. I didn't want to shop at all. Work is where I should be, waiting for that one call to come in, to help me catch Benny. He had been dormant for so long, but I knew deep in my soul he would resurface. Every case I took on was Benny; every victory a middle finger to Benny.

I got away.

I got away and I will get you, you bastard.

"So, what shop first?"

"I actually feel a headache coming on," I say with a groan, hoping she can't see through my lies. "Do you mind if we reschedule?" I rub my temple with the pads of two fingers for effect. She's used to my blow-offs by now and like a good parent, she lets me go.

"That's fine, honey," she says, lines of worry marring her forehead. "Go home and get some rest."

"I will," I say, though neither of us believe that lie.

Instead of going home, I find myself back at the precinct doing paperwork. My cell dings with a text message.

Detective Douche: $100 says you're working...

My partner likes to taunt me on weekends when I should be at home, but instead work old cases and go through old paperwork to make sure nothing was missed the first time around. He's an asshole. I type back with a smirk playing on my lips.

Me: I could use a new handbag.

I go to drop my phone back on the desk when it lights up again.

Detective Douche: HA! You carry your cash in your bra. I've never seen you with a handbag.

Dick.

Me: That's why I need one.

Ding.

Detective Douche: I'll be collecting my money Monday morning, Phillips.

Double dick.

"Phillips," Chief Stanton barks, startling me. Clicking my phone off and placing it in my desk, I give him my attention. It's late; I didn't realize just how late until I looked up from the computer. It's dark outside and my stomach grumbles for food.

"Chief," I nod.

He stops by my desk and leans into it. "Isn't today your day off?"

His white bushy eyebrows pinch together and he folds his arms over his chest, emphasizing the beer belly he has going on.

"I just wanted to make a few tweaks to a couple reports," I lie. *Always lying.*

He already knows how much time I spend here, so he must be bored if he's standing here breaking my non-existent balls.

"Here," he says, digging into his slacks and pulling out a twenty. He spends a couple seconds ironing out the creases between his fingers before offering it to me. "I can hear your hunger from here. Go get us some sandwiches from Benny's."

Benny.

Thud.

"What?" I breathe, a tremor rattling through my body.

"Jenny's Subs, across the street," he grunts and then frowns. "Why do you look so pale? She passed that last health code inspection. It was just hearsay about the rat." He shakes his head and waves his hand to dismiss me.

Jenny's not Benny's. Fuck. I hate how he still affects me.

"Actually, Chief, a homicide just came in. I could use her if that's cool with you," Detective Marcus says, walking past my desk.

Reaching over, Stanton snatches the twenty back and nods his head, gesturing for me to go with Marcus.

Charming. *Tight ass.*

"Why do you need me?" I ask as we pull up to a residential block. None of the detectives in the department like me that much, so him asking me to come along is unusual, to say the least.

"You'll see," he smirks.

My brows dip and I bite the inside of my cheek as I follow him past the buzzing of other residents in the building.

"We been tellin' you pigs for weeks he would kill her in the end and you didn't fuckin' listen," a woman yells, waving her hands around her head like she's swatting a wasp.

Pointing to the open door behind her, Marcus barks, "Get inside."

She "pffts" at him and remains parked where she can watch what we're up to.

Uniformed officers stand at the entrance to the scene of the crime.

"Get these people back in their homes and tell them we'll be around to take statements in due course," I tell the uniform who looks like he's going to vomit all over his sparkly black shoes. *Rookie.*

Pushing inside, there's noise and movement to my left where a kitchen is situated.

Two uniforms sit with a strong, built man in cuffs. He's shirtless with blood splatter all over his chest and face, demanding to be let go and shouting how it was an accident. His eyes clash with mine and I imagine steam coming from his nostrils as he breathes heavy and deep. In him, I see the same darkness Benny always had in his eyes—no remorse, lacking empathy.

My feet carry me into the living space where a naked woman lays on her back. I skim over her exposed flesh, logging everything that stands out. Contusions to her wrists, blue in color. She was tied up recently. New and old bruises on her inner thighs. Signs of rough sex or rape. Bruising around the throat shows signs of strangulation. Coloration suggests ante mortem and more than likely the cause of death. There is an injury to her head from blunt force trauma, supposedly from the fireplace, but the spray over the suspect in the other room and the little blood and lack of inflammation tells me this was caused after death.

Rolling my head on my shoulders, I pull a pair of latex gloves from my jacket pocket and snap them into place before making my way back through the small apartment to the kitchen. The suspect glares at me and chin lifts his head.

"It was an accident. She fell," he grits out.

"And the bruises?" I question, darting my eyes over him to study the splatter on his chest.

"We like to fuck," he says with a shrug. "Rough. She fucking loved it. I bet you would too." He licks his lips and smacks them at me before crinkling his nose. "Unless you're a fucking dike."

Because I'm a detective and don't walk around in girly shit? That's a new one. *Dick.*

"What did you use?" I ask, and his right eye twitches. "To smash her head in?" I clarify.

"She fell on the fireplace," he barks, his tone defensive.

A bitter laugh escapes me as I motion to the blood on his chest and face.

"I held her after," he counters.

"You're an idiot."

His body tenses at my insult.

"You're a woman beating, raping, piece of shit who strangled his girlfriend to death and then panicked. You waited while your peanut-sized brain could come up with a plan, found something to cave her head in with, and then left her by the fireplace."

I poke him in the chest and he heaves.

"The autopsy will show cause of death, idiot. But in the meantime, let me educate you. Blood doesn't clot after death, so it sprays differently, and without the body pushing it through the veins, it just sits in there instead of pumping out." Reaching for the back of his head, I use all my weight and force his face into the table, relishing the pop of his nose breaking.

"Motherfucking bitch, I'll kill you!" he shouts as blood gushes from his nose.

"You tripped, and you'll bleed more than she did." I smirk, waltzing back through to Marcus.

"She assaulted me. She assaulted me," he bellows.

"You tripped," both uniforms say in unison.

"There will be an object hidden somewhere he used after death," I bark out. "Maybe a heavy ornament or the bottom of a trophy. The throttling caused her death. I'm going to get a ride home."

Marcus knew I'd be volatile with the suspect, that's why he wanted me to come. He knows I hate violence against women more than anything else, but I wasn't their entertainment. I could do his freaking job for him; I wasn't sticking around for the cleanup.

Climbing into bed, I cuddle up to my boyfriend, Bo.

Bo Adams—the literal boy next door. When I was rescued and finally reunited with my folks, it was Bo who came to my emotional aid. My parents knew nothing of how to deal with my rage. I was furious we couldn't find her. Furious at myself. Furious with the police. Furious with my parents.

It was Bo who showed me how to channel that aggression.

He took me to my first self-defense class only three months after I came home. My head was still fucked and I was weak, but eventually, I became obsessed. Not only did I learn how to defend myself, I learned how to seriously beat some ass if it ever came to it after taking other classes like kickboxing.

He taught me how to shoot. First just soda cans out the back of his dad's old flatbed, but then we moved on to hunting and every kill became Benny in my eyes. Every squeeze of that trigger, the resistance, and then the kickback was gratifying. Each time, I fantasized about it penetrating his skin, blood, bone.

Bo let me channel that aggression, that hate, and what started as a friendship between he and I evolved into something more. Once I made the move to the city, Bo followed, getting a position here at the local college, and we've been living together ever since. He hates it when I work late and on weekends because this is all the time we get together and he isn't even conscious for it.

I'm a terrible girlfriend, but he simply can't see that.

Rolling onto my back, I stare up at the ceiling and will sleep to come, praying, just like every night, Benny will leave me the fuck alone.

Of course, my prayers fall on deaf ears.

He'll be with me the moment I close my eyes.

CHAPTER TWO

~ *American Rose* ~

"Missing person. White female. Fourteen years old. Last seen at Woodland Hills mall at three-thirty yesterday afternoon. Phillips? You ready to go?"

White female. Fourteen years old. His words echo in my mind, causing the hairs to rise on my neck.

"What are you? Twelve?"

"I'm fourteen, and I'm not a little kid!"

"Yeah," I bark, squeezing my eyes shut, "calm your shit, Scott." The age of the vic makes me shudder. It's a stark reminder of how I too was taken at that age. Forcing the memory back into the recesses of my mind, I give him a raised brow and a one-finger salute.

He grunts as he stalks off. The moment Chief Stanton assigned us to work together, Dillon has been agitated. We've been partners for eight months and he still treats me like I'm a thorn in his side. It might be because of my age, but I'm not sure. I was young to make detective, but I wasn't undeserving of it. I worked my ass off to get in a position where I could actually do something about the monsters of the world.

Benny.

And maybe I am a thorn in Dillon's side, and young, but I won't be treated like I don't matter. He doesn't hold authority over me like he seems to believe. I put the hours in; he won't even work weekends.

I'm Stanton's dream detective when it comes to solving tricky cases and finding the tiny details everyone else misses. When I'm pouring over the files and evidence, I'm in my element. The clues don't evade me. I make sense of the madness. *Because I've lived within it.*

It's the people I have a problem with.

People like Dillon Scott.

The gossip mill at the station is strong. I hear the whispers and see the looks as people pass me. They all know. Everyone knows I was abducted with my sister when I was fourteen and I somehow managed to escape when I was eighteen, leaving my then thirteen-year-old sister behind. Each person knows I nearly died the day I escaped when I was hit by a Ford pickup truck. Hell, it's in the system—they only have to seek the information out on their computer and it's all there for them to see. To make assumptions about me and talk in hushed voices over drinks at the bar…they're about as subtle as your boyfriend going down on you wearing a gas mask.

After the accident, I'd spent three weeks in a medical induced coma due to internal bleeding and swelling of my brain, and when I woke up, I remembered nothing.

I remembered Benny, or Benjamin…or whoever the fuck he really is, and him taking us. I remembered the way his slick skin felt on mine as he took what didn't belong to him late into the evenings. I remember in the beginning the way *she* cried every night until she fell asleep. The worst part of remembering are certain triggers that affect me in my everyday life. I can shoot a man who pulls a weapon on me, but I can't go to the bathroom in the middle of the night without a light on. The shadows taunt me; they watch me and hide the monsters that could be lurking there. I remember the deafening silence of my dream state. He stole everything from me in the end—even my dreams. I remember his scent, taste, height, how heavy he was when he pinned me to the small bed.

I just couldn't remember anything else.

The important stuff. Where I ran away from. How long I'd been running before the truck hit me. How long we drove from the flea market the day he took us. The make and model of his van. Branding on any food he gave us. Any sort of detail that could help. Police asked me these questions, and they were the same questions I've since asked many other victims throughout my time on the force.

It always leads to nothing.

The police canvased the area for miles from the accident. No house went unchecked. It was as if I appeared out of thin air.

And I've been looking for her ever since.

Until I find her, I do what I can to find other missing girls. They call me the tracker, in jest.

I'm ruthless and tend to bend rules when I need to in order to solve missing person cases.

Chief Stanton and Lieutenant Wallis are always on my ass for it. I've been written up more times than I can count for chasing rabbits without backup right into the lion's den. So far, I've been lucky, and I'll take all the luck I can get. I need it to find her. I'll never give up on her.

But my determined personality is what makes me go through partners like most people change their underwear. Nobody likes working with me. Dillon's lasted the longest, I'll give him that. He's a prick though and nobody likes partnering with him either. We're an unlikely pair.

The entire route to the mall, I wonder if this missing girl could be the link to finding my sister. It's how I treat each missing person case. With a fine tooth comb, I rake through the details until I shake out all the clues and leads. Our precinct leads the state on solved cases, and because of this, the woman with the most write-ups on her record also has the most accolades. It drives the boys in the department nuts.

I don't care about them, though. Or the awards.

I don't care if I get written up a thousand times.

All I care about is finding *them*.

Finding *her*.

I may have always wanted to be in the police force, but after *him*, after leaving her, I had to be. I needed the best position and resources at my disposal to help me hunt him down.

"This place has really gone to shit since the nineties. Back in my day, this mall was a respectable place to hang out. We were good kids and didn't get into any shit. Now, it's full of fuckin' gangsters. Look," Dillon points as he circles a group of mostly dark-skinned teens, "point made."

I roll my eyes as he stops the squad car. "You're a redneck racist, Scott. Those kids look like normal teens to me. You go inside and question the respectable people. I'll talk to the 'gangsters.'" I smirk at him, which earns me a muttered, "Fuck you, I wasn't referring to their skin color."

"If I get 'clipped' while you're inside, it was nice knowing you," I add, bringing my fingers up to my lips to mimic being afraid. He grumbles, but doesn't reward me with a reply as he stalks off. I approach the "gang" with purpose.

Find the girl.

"Detective Phillips. I'd like to ask you guys a couple questions," I say, revealing my badge on my belt.

A couple of the teen boys look nervous and hiss under their breath, but I'm not here to bust them for a little pot or whatever it is they're worried about. I only care about finding the girl.

Pulling my phone from my blazer pocket, I hold up a picture of the missing person. Alena Stevens. Her bright blue eyes haunt me. She's sweet and innocent. *Like I was.*

"Were you kids here yesterday?"

"Pfft…kids." One of the boys folds his arms and glares at me. "Yeah, so what? It's not a crime."

"Seen this girl?" I ask, holding up her image.

The group visibly relaxes and a girl with black hair slicked back into a ponytail steps forward. She smacks her gum and narrows her eyes. "Yeah, I think I saw her at Raze yesterday. She was trying on some glittery-ass pumps only white girls would be caught dead wearing." The group sniggers, all except a petite creamy-skinned girl holding hands with a boy the forthcoming girl can't keep her eyes off. I raise a brow at her.

"Do you have a sister?" I question, my voice gentle.

She tilts her head to the girl beside her who looks just like her. "Keisha, yeah. So?"

"Alena is someone's sister. Someone took her from

her family. The world is full of evil, vile people. Every second is precious in finding this girl. If it were Keisha, you'd want help too."

Her gaze softens and she glances at Keisha. "I saw her talking to a guy outside the store."

My interest piques and I flip open my pad. "Guy? Describe the guy."

"I don't know. Kinda cute, I guess, if you like Orlando Bloom." Her sister snickers and a cold chill washes over me.

"Please be more descriptive. What's your name?"

"Kiki."

"What did the man look like, Kiki? Was he young? Old? Did he have facial hair? What was he wearing?"

She plays with the hoop earring in her ear while looking over my face. "Maybe like your age. You know, old. He had curly brown hair. I guess he was cute. White girl thought so. Her face was bright-ass red and the girl was smiling so big, I thought she was planning their wedding in her head or some shit."

A shudder ripples through me. I remember the way he made me and Macy smile. How he wooed us right into his van. *It's him. It has to be him.* A sense of urgency and then blood curdling alarm trickles through my veins and settles in my heart. *Thud, thud, thud.* If it is him and he's looking for a new doll, what if he's finished with Macy?

"Can you tell me anything else? Did you hear them talking? Did he force her to go with him?" I bark, my height leering over her, causing her to lose some of the sass she held in her posture moments before. Her hand drops from her hip and cradles around her stomach.

She shrugs, but her voice holds a slight quiver. "He wasn't forcing her to do nothin'. She just nodded her head at whatever he said and followed him."

With a sigh, I force a smile even though I want to throw up. "Thanks. Anyone else see anything that can help us in our investigation?" I still don't have anything I can really work with—no trail to follow. Just a description that could be him, but also a thousand other men.

They all shake their heads and I try not to let the crush of defeat swallow me whole.

This isn't defeat; this still could be a lead. The perp sounds oddly like *him* and the behavior matches his MO.

I will find his ass eventually.

"There." I point to the image on the monitor from the mall's security footage. It's Alena leaving the store alone and a man matching the description Kiki gave follows less than a minute later. His head is down and he slips a baseball cap on to hide his face. "Can you alter the angle?" I demand.

"No, this is the only one that faces that part of the mall," the tech guy announces, playing around with buttons and bringing the lighting up a notch on the screen to better illuminate the picture. This room is small and stuffy as hell. It's claustrophobic for a mall this big and there has to be a hundred monitors in here. Dillon's huge frame crowds my own in the tiny space and every time I inhale, it's his exhale I'm filling my lungs with. He smells sweet like he's sucking on some candy. My stomach growls and I roll my eyes at the very thought of sweet and Dillon in the same thought.

"What about the exits?" Dillon asks, leaning over the guy's shoulder and brushing my arm as he does. An icy shiver runs through me despite the heat of the room. I don't do well in cramped spaces.

He types stuff into his computer and clicks on a file. "When you guys called this morning, I got straight on here and found the girl," he says, jabbing his finger at the screen. "That's her exiting the mall."

He shows us the girl on a different camera. She's leaving via the southwest parking lot and quickly goes out of view. The security guy lifts his hand to end the footage and I grab his wrist, stopping him. "Wait." Moments later, the man in the cap comes out.

My heart rate increases as I watch the man on the screen. He doesn't look big enough to be Benny, but it's been eight years since I last saw him. He could have lost weight and mass.

It's him. It has to be him.

"He goes a different direction," Dillon announces, dropping his gaze to my chest and then looking away. It's subtle, but I pick up on it straightaway. Heat floods through me which doesn't help my situation in this cramped room.

"Doesn't mean he didn't come back," I argue, fanning myself, "or cut her off a different way."

His head swivels back to me, dark brows pinched together as he scrutinizes me. "Or he's just a guy leaving the mall to go home."

There it is again. His stare drops to my chest and I look down to the spot he keeps gawking at. My mouth drops open and then closes as my skin burns on the edge of mortification. A button has come open and sweat glistens on my cleavage all out there for everyone to see. Fumbling with my jacket, I pull it closed over my shirt and risk overheating.

A smile plays at one corner his lips and he gives a slight shake of his head before he grows serious again. "He doesn't come back. It's just a guy," Dillon concludes, bringing his eyes to my face.

Just a guy my ass. Benny isn't just a guy—he's a monster.

A defeated huff leaves me. Dillon's right. We will need more than the evidence on the footage. Tapping the tech guy on the shoulder and gesturing with a pointed finger at the screen, I tell him, "Send these over to the precinct. It's evidence."

I leave Dillon and the man alone, eagerly escaping the suffocating room that reminds me all too much of a prison I lived in.

I'm coming for you, Benny.

"How was your day, babe?"

I drop my gun and badge on the table beside my purse and follow my nose into the kitchen where Bo is standing at the stove.

"Fine," I say with a sigh and pat his back as I peek into the skillet. "Hamburger steak, mmm." If he didn't cook for me, I would have starved to death a long time ago.

He chuckles and kisses the top of my head. "You look like hell today. So glad you came home. Are you sure everything is fine?" His brows lift in question.

"Just what I want to hear from the man who claims to love me," I tease, stealing a piece of celery from the bowl of salad he's prepared.

"I don't just claim it, baby. I'll show you it too, later." He winks and I internally sigh. He truly is a good man.

My eyes drag over his handsome face, taking in his sweet features. He doesn't have much facial hair, but what he does have matches his dark blonde, naturally shaggy hair he now keeps short because of me. The first night we slept together, when he cuddled into me from behind in the dark room and the strands tickled over my skin, I became hostage to a night terror of *him*—only I wasn't sleeping. I fought back, knocking Bo to the floor and leaving a scar above his right eye from a punch I threw while wearing the ring he had gifted me earlier that day. I was a mess back then, still am now, but he adores me. I feel it in his touch, when he gazes at me with those crystal blue eyes, and the way his smile lights up every room I darken. We truly do match—his good-naturedness with my chipped shoulder. The universe made sure we evened things out.

"Actually," I tell him with a huff as I go on the hunt for plates, "it was terrible. Missing person. Alena Stevens. Fourteen."

Taken from the mall by him.

He turns off the stove, but doesn't say anything, and I sense the shift in his mood. Bo hates my obsession with finding Macy. He knows I treat each and every case like a lead to find her, and this one is no different. Telling him anything about the case is frowned upon, but if I didn't have him to vent to, I'd silently go insane.

"Try not to get sucked in, babe. You tend to lose too

much weight and not sleep enough. I like my girl on the curvy side," he says with a forced grin. He always tries to make light of my fucked up obsessions.

"Well, I'm starving, so your curvy girl isn't changing any time soon."

This time, I earn myself a genuine grin from the good looking man.

"Good. I like you just the way you are."

And he did. I was fairly attractive, I suppose. The mirror showed me I'd blossomed into an appealing woman during those years I was locked away being used and abused by Benny. My dark locks complimented my pale complexion and my hazel eyes that mirrored Macy's were vibrant but jaded. My figure was only now beginning to have curves that showed I was a woman. It took years for Bo to put meat on my fragile bones and I liked the fuller hips I now owned. They flattered my modest C cup and rounded ass.

I guess there's a reason Bo is in love with me—and it can't be my delightful personality.

But you don't love him.

I wake to lips sucking on my nipple and my heart jackknifes through my chest. For a split second, I'm back in my cell. I'm seventeen and he's taking me for the first time. It isn't until I thread my fingers into his hair that I realize I'm latching onto short, stick-straight hair—not curly, thick hair. My tense body tightens for a different reason as I embrace the feeling of his hot tongue circling and sucking.

"It's me, babe," he whispers. "It's just me."

Bo.

Sex isn't something I ever thought I'd want after Benny. I didn't like the way my body betrayed me with him, but Bo took things slow and taught me how to be in control of what I do and whom I share myself with. Sex is good with Bo. He's a gentle lover, but there's this demon lurking inside me, tainted by Benny's torture, that wants more—needs more.

"I love you. It's just me," he murmurs against my flesh as he trails kisses over the globe of my breast to my abdomen. "Don't ever forget that, babe."

I won't. I can't. There are many reasons why I hate myself and him loving me is one of them.

I don't deserve him.

I let out a whimper as his tongue dips into my belly button. He continues his tasting until I feel his hot breath against the sensitive lips of my pussy. A choked gasp escapes me the moment his tongue slides along my slit.

"I love you," he breathes against me, the three words hot as his breath scorches over my already fevered flesh. His mouth gives me the pleasure I need, but the words darken the spark that should be firing right now, causing my blood to chill.

He loved me too...

When I got with Bo, I wasn't looking for love. I was looking for a friend. The idea of being alone scared the shit out of me. Plus, Bo was what I should have been interested in all those years ago. He was headed for college with a good head on his shoulders. Instead, I allowed my stupid hormones to lead me right into a van that drove me straight to hell.

Never again will I let my body make decisions for me.

From now on, my mind calls all the shots. And love is something locked in a cell with my sister. I loved her more than anything, and I failed her. Love has no place in my life now.

"I love you, Jade. It's me, Bo," he murmurs again as he worships me between my legs. He reminds me every time he's inside me that it's him. I adore him for wanting me to feel safe in our moments of passion, but he doesn't realize Benny used to whisper those same three words.

Talking dirty would serve him and me better.

"I love you." His words are on repeat.

Shut up…shut up…shut up…

Sometimes I want to give in, tell him I love him too so he'll stop saying the words, gift him what he deserves, but I can't. I'm not a liar when it comes to such important things. Love is a lie.

"You're my sweet, adored Bo," I whisper. It's what I always tell him—my equivalent to his heartfelt words.

And he knows this.

Satisfied with my answer, he becomes ravenous, but I know he is still holding back, and I hate it.

He sucks and licks me like he's taken courses on how to do so. And being an anatomy teacher at the local college, who knows? Maybe he teaches the damn course. But sometimes, I wish he'd bite me. Hurt me just once.

"Yes," I moan as he slides a finger into my wet center. "More…"

He expertly finds the sweet spot within and soon, I'm shuddering with bliss. Bo knows how to make me orgasm.

So did Benny.

My body is a slut for pleasure and with Bo, it is punishment to myself as much as it's gratification. His words take me back there, yet his scent and touch keep me here. I'm in limbo.

And I deserve to be for not loving him back. How could I love him when I couldn't even give him my entire mind during sex?

Dirty little doll.

My thighs cage him to me until they weaken and fall to the sides.

"Jade…" His voice cracks with emotion as he climbs over me, spreading my legs farther apart so he can settle between them, the tip of his hardened cock teasing at my throbbing wet pussy.

"Mmm?"

Slowly, almost torturous, he drives into my needy body and I cry out when he pushes all the way inside.

"Babe…"

"Mmm?"

He thrusts harder and then sucks on my bottom lip. "Marry me."

An icy shower of reality douses the heated flames of my desire. His lips find my neck and he suckles as if I'm the most precious thing he's ever encountered. I can't marry him. I don't even love him. It's not his fault. Bo is the textbook partner. A great lover. Understanding and forgiving.

In a perfect world, I could love Bo—should. My parents love Bo, everyone freaking loves Bo…*but me.*

Perhaps if Benny had never stolen his pretty little

dolls, I'd have fallen for Bo.

But this isn't a perfect world.

He did steal us.

The world is wicked and hateful. I'll never stop searching for my sister. I'll never lose the desire to find all the missing girls in this world. I will never lose the festering hate for Benny and the all-consuming desire to bring him to justice.

There's just not enough room inside my broken heart for Bo. Bo is a good soul and my job, my desire for vengeance, will dirty him.

Bo's fingers on my clit between us jolts me from my thoughts. He works me into another delicious orgasm within minutes. When my body contracts around his modest cock, he releases his own climax into me. The moment our bodies still and our breathing is all that breaks the silence of the room, he lifts up to look down at me.

Moonlight shines on his handsome features, but I don't see the bright, happy man I know. All I see is sadness and loss. He wants more than I can give.

"Is that a no?" His Adam's apple bobs in his throat. I hate that I'm so toxic for him.

"Bo..." Tears prick my eyes, but they never fall. Not anymore. After what I've been through, nothing makes me cry. Not even a sad, broken man whose only wish in this world is for me to love him. "I would be a terrible wife."

"Not to me," he assures, his lips finding mine. "To me, you're pretty perfect."

Pretty little doll.

He kisses me so sweetly, I think my black heart might throb a little with life. It guts me for him.

"Okay," I murmur with a sigh, knowing I'll later regret it.

Dirty little doll.

"But I want a long engagement. Like a year or two." Cruel, selfish woman. I hate me.

His blue eyes shimmer in the moonlight and he grins. He truly is a beautiful soul. "I'll give you all the time you need, babe. We've got nothing but time."

I return his smile, but it doesn't reach my eyes.

He and I may have lots of time for *us*.

But I'm afraid Macy doesn't have much time at all.

If the man from the mall is Benny, that means he's on the hunt again. If he's on the hunt, then he's growing bored with his little dolly.

Or worse, maybe he's replacing a doll who's too broken to repair.

I have to find her.

And soon.

CHAPTER THREE

~ *Burgundy* ~

IT'S SO BRIGHT AND BIG.

Shiny and new.

Flawless.

Not me at all.

It's heavy and certainly not suitable for work. Dragging the engagement ring from my finger and dropping it onto the dresser top, I cringe at the fact that I agreed to marry Bo. I was selfish and petrified of losing him, so I became one of those women I despise by locking him in, knowing I can't give him everything he deserves, everything he's earned by just putting up with my shit-storm of a life.

"Does it need resizing?" His voice lures me from my inward disgust with myself.

"It's—"

"Perfect and pretty?" He flashes me a panty-melting grin. "Just like you."

Pretty little doll.

I suppress a shudder and force a smile.

His arms reach around my waist and clasp together to keep me locked against the hard planes of his chest. Bo eventually did grow muscle, and he works hard at the gym to maintain it. He's the ultimate dream for any woman. *Any woman but me.*

Spinning in his arms, I wrap mine around his neck and devour his lips with my own. Pushing past the threshold into his warm inviting mouth, I swipe and duel with his tongue until his cock strains against the apex of my thighs and he lifts me onto him. My legs snake around his waist and he breathes against my lips. "You'll be late."

I reply by grinding my pussy against him and biting down on his lip, and he rewards me with orgasms that make me forget my guilt.

Dillon hovers near my desk with his mug of black coffee that makes his breath smell like a barista threw up in his mouth after eating coffee beans straight from the plant. Looking at his watch and giving me the evil eye with a shake of his head, he says, "You're late."

"Eat another doughnut and stop stalking my timesheet," I quip, giving him a faux smile and double salute with both hands.

"Real mature, and stereotypical," he complains. "Seriously?"

The fucking sugar is still on the side of his mouth. Reaching out, I swipe the dust from the corner of his bottom lip and hold it up for him to see. His posture is rigid. Boundary issues are a problem for me. "Don't be a girl," I pfft, and then suck the sugar from my finger. It's not often I allow myself sugary treats. I shove away the box of half-eaten doughnuts I didn't put on my desk and quirk a brow. Pointing back to his face and shaking my head, I say, "No one needs to be a detective to solve this mystery."

He swipes at his mouth with the back of his hand and then places his mug on my file, leaving a dirty amber ring. I move it and shove it back at him. *Dick.*

"Any news on the missing girl?" I ask, hoping some new evidence came to light while we were sleeping.

He nods and points to a board that has all the cases pinned to it behind me. "The girl's mother came forward and said they had an argument before she went to the mall. We could be looking at a runaway."

"Why wouldn't she tell us this before?" I demand.

He shrugs and reaches for another doughnut. "She didn't want us not to look for her."

Of course we would look for her.

"Phillips, Scott, get in here," Lieutenant Wallis barks, signaling us with a hand wave before disappearing into his office.

"What have you done now?" I growl, knocking his last bite of doughnut from his hand.

"Bitch," he hisses to my retreating form before bending down and picking the dough blob up. "Five second rule," he barks. *Gross.*

"Close the door, Scott," Wallis orders, collapsing into his leather chair behind the desk. "I have a homicide that just came in. Chief wants you *both* on it."

"What about the missing person?" I say, a little too much need in my tone, gaining me a narrowed glare from Wallis. "Jones and Henderson will take over that case. She's more than likely a runaway who will be getting hungry and remorseful and return before the day is out. I need you two to work this case." He shoves a folder across the desk and gestures toward the office door. Grabbing the file before my partner can, I march from his office and mumble under my breath, "This is bullshit." I didn't mind taking lead on a homicide, but that girl was still out there, by choice or not. What if she was waiting to be found and rescued, but no one came looking for her?

"Let's go," Dillon orders, walking to my desk and reaching for the last doughnut. Jogging to keep up with his wide strides, I smack the fried goody from his grasp and grab it up for myself. He swipes up his jacket and smirks over his shoulder at me.

"We're heading out," he says, stating the obvious into the room at no one in particular.

Getting there before uniform officers trample all over the crime scene is paramount, so I follow Dillon out, taking one last glance at the photo of fourteen-year-old Alena Stevens tacked to the board before indulging in the doughnut, just to stop him from enjoying it. *Bitch.*

As we pull up to the location where a shop owner has been murdered in her store, my insides quake and my movements slow. It's almost like dirt inside my veins has solidified into concrete and I'm fighting to breathe.

Porcelain dolls decorate the shop window, all neat in a symmetrical space, glorifying their beauty. *Thud, thud, thud.*

Pretty little dolls...

"Phillips?"

A shudder threatens to ripple through me, but I somehow manage to keep it at bay. Jerking my eyes to his,

I nod a little too quickly. "I'm fine, I'm okay…I'm good," I stutter, and his brows crash together as he studies me with dark, intense eyes. They're not Benny dark, though. They swirl with caramel and behind the asshole I know on the outside, his eyes tell me there's a gentler version inside.

He's still staring at me and I realize I'm locked in his gaze, staring right back.

"I swear." I hold my hands up, breaking the spell.

He scrutinizes me for another long moment. "I was going to tell you to hurry the fuck up, not ask how the hell you're doing. Who do I look like, your damn boyfriend?"

A tiny *o* forms at my lips as I realize I just lost my shit in front of my partner. I've got to get a handle on my nerves or Dillon's going to have a heyday ripping me apart until he finds what's messing with my head. I shake the tension in my muscles away and glare at the asshole I'm grateful for right now. He smirks at my narrowed eyes aiming right at his.

"Come on," he says in a sugary-sweet sarcastic tone, "Big D'll hold your hand, pretty little thang." When I shudder, this time at his words, he laughs. "Don't worry," he says, his tone turning serious, "these things creep me the hell out as well."

"They don't creep me out," I counter.

It's what they represent that has my blood running cold.

He watches me and I squirm in my seat.

"Keep telling yourself that," he says in a smug tone before getting out of the car.

"Eat shit," I retort, exiting the vehicle with him.

He rubs his stomach and there's no evidence of his

sweet tooth showing on his trim waist and narrow hips. "I'm actually quite full."

"You ate nearly an entire box of baked goods," I huff, "I'm not surprised. You'll probably have a heart attack any minute."

The smirk on his face remains. "Then you'll have to give me mouth to mouth."

"Spit in your mouth is more like it."

"Stop flirting with me, Phillips," he says with a chuckle. "I don't want to share your bodily fluids right now. We have a homicide, show some respect."

My mouth drops as the urge to punch that smug grin right off his face takes over and I have to ignore the buzzing in my gut at his choice of words. He strides toward the shop with purpose and I dip my head to hide my own slight smile. I've never really looked at him before; never delved beyond the prickly surface. He's not bad looking, I suppose—when he's acting like a normal human being. *Liar*. Lying to myself is impossible. Dillon is hot, raw, and alpha in every way, but all that hotness is eclipsed with his snotty attitude toward me.

"Are you checking me out?" Stopping at the entrance of the shop, he looks back at me, ignoring the flurry of activity. A crowd had formed beyond the taped off area and despite being told to stay out of the crime scene every damn time a homicide happens, a uniformed officer is staring out at us from the store with a body by his feet. *Freaking idiots*.

"I was, actually," I mutter before stalking toward my crime scene. "I was checking out the best angle of your ass to kick you up."

"Ass play? Now that surprises me." He shrugs and leaves me open-mouthed once more, staring after his retreating form.

He momentarily distracted me from the horrors this place holds and it's unclear whether that was on purpose or not. But now, without his playful taunting, it crashes down around me like a ton of bricks.

Everyone knows what happened to you, dirty little doll.

My lungs burn and beg for air as I hold my breath and enter the shop. They're everywhere, glaring at me from the shelves, from the cabinets. Pale skin, ruby red lips, wide eyes staring right through to my marrow.

"Jade?"

My eyes snap up to his. *Dillon said my name.* My first name. Eight months I've worked cases with him, sat beside him in the car, ate at the same table, and not once has he used my first name. I hold his gaze, allowing it to keep me anchored.

"You should go talk to the witness outside in the patrol car." My eyes travel down to the woman slain and discarded on the floor, blood pooled around her. She didn't see it coming. The blood spray on the counter shows he came up behind her. There's nothing broken or any signs of struggle.

Crash!

Startled, my whole body jolts from the sound of porcelain hitting the wooden floor and shattering. My heart thunders as blood rushes through my veins and pounds in my ears. I track the sound with my eyes to the now broken doll lying next to the shop owner.

The officer who shouldn't be here in the first place

stares down at the mess. His nose scrunched, he brings a fist to his mouth and bites down before folding his arms. "Err, it slipped," he says, turning his head to the shelving unit behind him. *Idiot.*

Her dismantled face in shards stares up at me and my memories swallow me.

The thunder growling from the sky and the hissing of the rain hitting the wall outside is soothing.

I imagine the water building and flooding into my cell, drowning me, releasing me from this burden of a life.

Macy is sniffling and every time the lightening crackles in the air, she screeches.

I wish I could see the color of the bolt, smell the scent of the rain, and experience the night air on my skin. Time passes, but I stopped keeping track of the notches I made on the wall when my fingernail ripped off while trying to etch a line for day thirteen.

That was so long ago now.

My hair is longer and my chest finally filled out. If only Bo could see me now, he wouldn't make fun of me for being flat-chested.

Momma used to say boys who were mean just liked you and didn't know how to express it, and I suppose in a way she was right. Benny is cruel, but he claims he loves us.

Crackle…boom. "Argh."

Smash!

A gasp rings out from beyond the wooden panels of my cell door as a stampede of horses rattle in my ribcage.

"Look what you made me do!" Benny—Benjamin

roars. Tiny bumps break out over my skin as an icy quiver snakes up my spine and over my shoulders, rooting itself within my chest.

"She's ruined." His voice drops low, almost childlike. A clanking sounds out and I rush to the latch in my door left open for me to view him outside working on his dolls.

"It's my fault," I declare, trying to sway him into unlocking my door and giving me Macy's punishment. My voice finds only silence in return, and it's earsplitting. There's nothing but the anger of the storm raging outside.

Until the screams from Macy's lips fire into me like bullets made of venom, poisoning my once innocent heart.

Placing my hands on the battered wood of the door, splinters dig into my fingernails, causing blood to bubble on the tips. Air rushes out of me like someone pushed through my stomach and squeezed my lungs into dust.

Hard, chiseled muscle flexes under a mist of sweat on his bare back as he leans over a huddled form caught in his grasp by her hair.

Layers of thick, brown hair curtain around her face.

He brought her outside her cell.

My mind reels in disbelief.

I haven't glimpsed my sister since the day he stole us.

"Look what you did," he growls. "She's broken. She was a pretty little doll just like you and now she's ugly."

Reaching down, he picks up a shard of porcelain with his free hand, then straightens to his full height, which almost reaches the light bulb dangling from the ceiling, bringing Macy up with him. She reaches up onto her tiptoes and the frilly dress she's wearing ruffles and sways with her movements.

When her hair falls away from her face, I truly see her for the first time in so long. Hot tears burn in my eyes, brimming my lashes. She's different, but the same. My heart is happy to see her, yet my soul is sad.

I didn't keep her safe.

"Tell her you're sorry," he rages, his entire body quaking with anger. "Cry for the broken dolly." When she doesn't speak, he raises his hand. At first, I fear he'll hit her and the blood in my body stops pumping altogether as I wait for his impending blow.

But then, softly, almost gently, he does something worse.

Clutching one of the porcelain shards in his grip, he pokes it into her flesh just below Macy's tear duct with steady movements.

Bile rises in my throat as blood blooms around the creamy porcelain. A scream threatens to suffocate me as he drags the sharp edge down along the side of her nose, the shard creating a crimson river in its wake. Her lips part, but she doesn't cry out. Instead, her eyes meet his, and they flicker with sorrow. Her bottom lip quivers and in a meek, regretful tone, she tells him, "I'm sorry."

I find my voice—louder than the thunder crashing outside—and yank at the metal on my cage. "Let her go, you maniac!"

He remains frozen in the sick, twisted position of holding my sister by the throat as her face bleeds. Just staring. Always staring. I ball my hands into fists and hammer them against the door, hoping to drag his attention away from her, all to no effect. Her hazel eyes flicker to mine and I sob so hard, my chest hurts.

"Forgive me, Macy. I'm so sorry...forgive me. I'm going

to save us, I promise."

My will loses fight as my knees buckle and I nearly fall to the floor, screaming alongside the storm, hoping it will carry me away when it eventually passes, leaving behind the merciless heat. He disappears with my sister into her cage and I feel powerless in my world. I bury my face in my sweaty, dirty palms.

"Miss Polly had a dolly who was sick, sick, sick.

So she phoned for the doctor to be quick, quick, quick."

He reemerges from her cell singing his creepy song while picking up the pieces of his broken doll outside our cells. She will never go back to being his pretty doll again. Just like Macy will now forever bear his jagged mark on her face. Just like I will never be able to hide the cracks he has created within me.

I know from hearing his song he won't visit my cell tonight, or my sister's. Thank God. He will leave us and tomorrow we won't get fed. But at least we'll get a reprieve from the monster who holds our destiny in the palm of his wicked hand.

"Jade, what the hell are you humming? Are you sure you want to be in here?"

My eyes snap to Dillon's, but the memory hangs thick in the air. I can almost taste the dust from my cell. Almost smell Benny's familiar scent lingering like a cloying fog. "Humming?"

He shakes his head and eyes me like I've lost my mind. "Yeah, some creepy-ass tune."

Too afraid to touch on the fact that Benny is still with me, I ignore him and glare at the uniform. "Anything else you want to do to disturb the crime scene? Maybe sit and play in her blood?" I snap, gesturing to the door with a stern finger. "Show me where the witness is."

I follow the stuttering officer out, ignoring the burning gaze at my back.

This has Benny written all over it.

He's here.

He took that girl. He wants a new doll.

Why this shop? Killing a woman of this age for no reason isn't his MO. He was premeditated when it came to taking a girl. Murdered when enraged. Has he evolved? Did he need supplies? Was he really back?

CHAPTER FOUR

~ Magenta ~

"Are you Madison Kline?"

The twenty-something woman nods, her eyes wide with fright. "Is it true? Is Mrs. Hawthorne..." her voice croaks, "d-dead?"

I look to the store window a few feet away from where I brought her outside the tape to get some privacy from the thickening crowd. One of the medical examiners is standing with his back to us, staring down at the body. His hand motions to the wound on her neck as he says something to his partner. Dragging my eyes back to the woman, I let out a sigh.

"I'm afraid so. I'm going to need to ask you some questions."

She nods, a small, wobbly frown at her lips, but her now teary eyes stay trained on the window. "Who would do such an awful thing? Mrs. Hawthorne was the nicest person. She made dolls for crying out loud. It's not like we even sold enough for anyone to rob us. I just don't understand."

I reach for her and grip her shoulder. "Some people are evil, Miss Kline. We may not understand their reasoning." Releasing her, I give her a grim smile. "The best we can do now is catch the man who did this."

Her brows furrow together. "Man?"

Heat floods my cheeks and I swallow. "Person," I rush out, correcting myself.

Although homicides are committed by men over eighty percent of the time, it was still a slip that shouldn't have happened.

Benny.

"We're going to catch the perpetrator. Now, can you tell me where you were between the hours of eight and midnight last night?"

Miss Kline nods. "At home. I took a shower around eight. Watched television until about ten before going to bed. Why?"

"Can anyone corroborate your statement?" She's not a suspect, I'm simply doing due diligence.

"My ma. I still live at home."

I cast my gaze down to my notebook while I scribble information for my report later when she steps past me, her fingertip touching the glass of the shop window.

Turning my head, I watch her as she stares inside. I half expect her to burst into tears at seeing the body from the window, but she jerks her tearstained face to mine instead, pointing to the row of dolls up front.

"This wasn't here yesterday. It's not one of ours."

My body tenses as I follow her finger. At the end sits a boy porcelain doll. Messy brown hair. Overalls. A sad frown on his face.

I know this doll.

Benny.

She continues to speak, but I'm frozen in place, in

the sweltering heat of the flea market once again. I'm with Benny and Macy. I'm packing the boy doll I want carefully into the box, promising him my dad will buy him, that everything will be okay and he'll be mine soon.

I even broke my promise to a stupid doll.

"Stop crying," he warns, regarding me through the bars, his tone hard, nothing like the man from the market.

"The papers say you're fourteen."

"I am. You know this, I told you."

He studies me through the bars separating us. "I assumed you were older," he muses to himself.

I assumed he was sane. I guess we were both wrong.

"Let me go! What have you done to Macy?" I demand, swiping at my tears.

"Nothing. She's playing with her doll." He unlocks the latch in the door and the bars usually blocking the space between us pull open in his hands. With a grunt, he pushes a doll through the gap.

My breath hitches on a hiccup. It's the one from his booth—the boy doll I wanted.

"Here, have your dolly," he tells me, gently shaking it at me.

Anger coils in my gut and I run toward the door, snatching the doll from his hand.

"I don't want your stupid doll," I scream, tearing at the doll's hair and clothes before throwing it on the bed. When I run back to the latch, he's glaring down at the mess I've made of his precious doll.

Good.

I already told him before I was too old for his stupid dolls.

"Let me out. I want to go home," I bellow, tiptoeing to see into his face through the open latch.

Cold abyss stares back at me, choking me in its darkness, like it's penetrating my body, obscuring me from the inside out.

A hand too quick for me to stop reaches in and grabs me around the throat, squeezing.

My eyes expand in shock, the blood vessels screaming for mercy.

A shriek attempts to escape me, but it's without sound. He's so strong. I claw at the hand stealing my life, but it's having no effect. He remains stoic, staring in at me, his grip gaining strength.

I'm fading…dying…stop.

Air rushes into my lungs, scorching my raw gullet as I'm released. I drop to the floor and pain slices into my kneecaps, shooting up my body.

Clank.

"No," I choke past the rawness scratching my throat, crawling away from the door that's now opening. His shadow creeps over me like a dark tide—infecting me, overwhelming me, drowning me.

A hand grips my hair, dragging me to my feet while my legs flail beneath me. My follicles are set ablaze, the pain spanning my entire scalp.

"Stop, please," I beg, my voice broken and hoarse. "I want to go home."

"This is *home now," he tells me, not one inflection of emotion in his voice. So matter of fact.*

He yanks me back and I fall onto the bed, his clenched fist gripping strands of my hair. When he draws his gaze to the boy doll, my eyes follow and a whimper leaves me.

I pulled tufts of the hair out and ripped the clothes from the little doll.

Slow and menacing, he drags his eyes back to me. My head shakes no as my body trembles and cowers. Heavy hands grab at me, tearing my clothes. I fight, lashing at him with a frenzied bout of energy and fury. Humiliation, pain, and fear saturate my soul as he subdues me without any effort, leaving me in my bra and panties when he's finished, embarrassed and terrified.

Picking up the doll, he walks out as I curl into the fetal position, traumatized with the reality seeping into my heart.

I wasn't going home ever...

Nothing was ever going to be okay again.

"Detective?"

Her voice jerks me from the past and my words choke me as I try to get them out. When a large, firm hand grips my shoulder, I cry out in surprise.

Benny.

My body moves on the instincts I've worked hard to build into it; my muscles coil and the kickboxing lessons come into play. Extending my arm and spinning around with my fist reared back, I prepare to slam it into his nose, my thoughts on my gun. I need it to put holes into him he will never recover from—ending this turmoil growing inside me, haunting my life.

As soon as my fist flies toward the figure of the man,

confusion causes me to hesitate briefly. It's enough of a pause that he has time to grab my wrist and twist it behind my back, forcing my body forward. Our chests touch as I fall against him, using my free hand to steady myself so my face doesn't crash against the hard planes of his physique. My whole body quakes with terror, until his scent invades my senses and the heavy pounding of his pulse causes his heart to thump against the palm of my hand. It matches my own, battering against my ribcage, trying to tear free and put an end to it all.

Dillon.

"Jade," he hisses, his hot breath tickling my face. "It's me, Dillon. What the hell is going on with you?"

Fat tears well in my eyes upon realizing I lost my shit in front of the person I've been questioning, and worse, my partner. I don't let the tears spill and bite my lip to keep it from wobbling. "Nothing's wrong," I murmur, pulling my arms free and cradling them around myself so I don't throw them around him just for some human comfort right now. I feel weak; Benny's winning.

His dark eyes narrow as he scrutinizes my face up close. I've never noticed Dillon has freckles. Or that his eyes hold sad secrets. I never noticed he smells like leather and something contradictory—peppermint, maybe? "Take a lunch break," he says, his tone gruff. "When I wrap up here, we're going to talk about this." He releases me from his probing gaze and stalks back toward the shop.

Before he goes in, I shout, "Detective Scott."

Turning, he regards me as if I'm a mystery he wants to solve. He'll never figure me out. Hell, I can't even figure myself out.

"Bag the boy doll. Check for prints. Miss Kline says it wasn't here yesterday."

It's him. *I know it's him.*

Looking to the doll and then back at me, his eyes narrow and he doesn't move. He must sense my hesitation. He knows I want to say more.

"What else?" he questions, his massive frame blocking the doorway.

"I think it's *him*." The words are spoken before I can stop them and I wish I could shove them back into my mouth.

He'll think I'm crazy. He'll tell Chief Stanton he wants a new partner.

"Him as in…" he starts, but I wave him off and stalk toward the squad car.

I have to get away from here.

I have to think.

Benny is so close, I can taste it. He's back and I'm going to end him.

I've been circling the block for twenty minutes. Dillon sent me away to clear my mind and it's clear. Crystal clear. It's imperative I speak with the mother of the missing girl. I know these cases are connected. I can feel it in my bones. It's too much of a coincidence.

When her house comes into view again, I let out a rush of breath. I'll probably get written up for disobeying orders again, but I won't be able to sleep until it's done. I need to talk to her.

To possibly warn her of the severity of her situation.

Truth is, she may never get her daughter back.

A shuffling and scraping sound rouses me from slumber.
He's back.

A grunt and then a thump has my curiosity piqued.

Slipping from the sheet he allows me to have, I creep across my cell and peek through the bars, my breath hitching when I see him there.

He's not alone.

There's a woman lying on his table, naked and unconscious. Sensing his movements, I quickly drop my knees to duck when he turns and walks past my cell toward the doorway leading to my freedom at the far left wall of our prison.

My heart thuds manically in my chest and there's an excited flurry in my stomach I haven't felt in a long time—one I thought I'd never feel again.

"Hey," I hiss. "Hey, you," I try again a little louder, keeping my eyes between her and the doorway.

Movements sound from Macy's cell and she whispers, "Who is that?"

"Hey, lady." I try rapping my hands on the wood panel of my cell door.

She stirs, her hand reaching up to rub at her head as she shifts to a sitting position. She's not a lady at all. She's a girl. Older than me, but still a girl—maybe nineteen, twenty.

"What happened?" she questions, her voice a thick slur, groggy sounding. Her dark hair curtains around her face as she dips her head to look down at the floor and then back up. Our eyes clash—hers confused and mine worried.

Her eyes widen and she jumps down to her feet, swaying a little. "What the fuck is happening? Who are you?" *she demands, panic in her tone and volume.* "Why am I naked?" *This time, her voice wobbles with terror.*

She isn't here willingly.

She's a new doll.

"Shhh," *I hush, pointing to the doorway. Her head swivels to where I gesture and she shakes it no before wobbling over to the bars separating us.*

"Where are we? Why are you in there? Who is he?" *she demands, her words rising in pitch with each question.*

Footsteps sound from nearby and then his shadow creeps up the wall of the open doorway.

"Don't look, Macy. Get into your bed," *I whisper-yell. The air is thick and a stirring in my stomach tells me she shouldn't see what's about to happen.*

Neither should I…

Each step he takes toward us peels with it a piece of my soul.

The girl flattens her back against my cell door. "Stay away from me," *she screams at him, holding her hands out in front of her.*

"Run," *I urge. But we both know there's nowhere to run.*

Cowering, her body scrapes across the door as his impending form strides toward her. With courage that bursts from somewhere deep within her, she launches at him, scratching at his face. He hisses and backhands her across her cheek, contacting with a stomach-lurching crunch. I gape in horror as her head jerks to the side like it's attached to a spring and connects with my door, making it vibrate against my body.

She screams and he growls in response.

Glowering at her, he fingers the scratch she made on his face. Blood smears across his cheek and it makes him all the more menacing.

My hands turn white from gripping the bars so tight and start to lose feeling. "Stop, please," I beg for her, but I've seen that look before in his eyes. I've been the cause of it and withstood the punishment...barely.

She gains her stability and lifts her head to look directly at me. Blood pours from her nose and she spits a tooth from her mouth, gurgling on the torrent of it. It's like a crimson waterfall from her lips. She turns to face her new master and the indifference he shows falters as he begins grinding his teeth.

"Look what you've done!" he bellows, grasping her jaw between his thumb and forefinger.

Benny yanks her across the room by her chin, her feet tripping and dragging to keep up. His hand grips the back of her head as he forces her to look in a mirror stained with rust around the frame adorning the wall opposite my cell.

"You're not a pretty doll anymore," he growls, pushing her head forward so she can see better. With a quick motion, he pulls her head back before ramming her forward once more.

The sickening sound causes bile to rise in my throat. Someone screams and it takes me a minute to realize the horrified noise is coming from me.

Over and over again, he smashes her face against the mirror. The crunching sound of her head hitting and bones crushing under the force of his strength and then just splats causes vomit to burst from my mouth, spraying out in front of me.

It is the most disgusting and truly terrifying act I've ever witnessed, yet I still can't tear my gaze. Blood coats every inch of him. Benny is a predator who just annihilated his prey. With an aggravated huff, he lets her lifeless body drop to the floor with a thump. He cracks his neck and then slowly swivels his head around, his dark, enraged eyes meeting mine.

The predator is still hungry.

A scream lodges in my throat as he advances, but dies before it can escape. Fear drives me to drop to the floor and wait for the monster pacing outside my cell. I pray he'll sing—singing will save Macy and me from his wrath.

Dragging myself back to the present, I take a deep breath in before pulling over and stopping the car with a screech of the brakes. Before I can change my mind, I'm already stalking up toward the small, one-story home with the shutters hanging off the windows. What Benny is capable of fuels me on, charging me forward.

Clomping up the front steps, I try to calm my nerves, to take deep breaths like my stupid psychiatrist used to have me do while in our sessions.

Breathe, Jade.

You're this girl's only help.

She might be the key to getting Macy back.

I'm about to rap on the door when it flies open. A woman with frizzy blonde hair and bags under her eyes regards me with an expectant look.

"Did you find Alena?"

My shoulders hunch and I shake my head. "Not yet, but I promise we're doing everything we can to find your daughter."

Tears well in her eyes as she nods. "Please, come inside."

I follow her into the house and take a seat in the living room. She sits in the recliner, her eyes on a photograph of Alena on the end table.

Alena is younger in the photo, maybe nine or ten. She clutches a doll with red, raggedy hair.

Pretty little doll.

Tearing my gaze from the picture, I return my attention to the woman. "Did Alena have any boyfriends? Was she ever disobedient? Did you have a falling out?"

Mrs. Stevens shakes her head and clasps her long fingers together in her lap. "No, she was a bit awkward for her age. Never had any interest in boys as far as I could tell. She always did as she was told. A good girl, my daughter."

This confirms my suspicions.

Macy and I were good girls too.

"Do you have any idea who could have taken her?" I question.

She shakes her head. "I don't know. You think someone has taken my baby?"

Benny.

"We don't know that yet, but we need to look at all possibilities."

It was Benny.

I'm dying to say as much, but bite my tongue. Instead, I pull out a copy of the sketched image I shoved into my pocket from my desk before I left the station earlier.

A sketch from when I woke up from that coma all those years ago and explained in detail what Benny looked like. The sketch artist did an eerily good job on making Benny come back to life. I'd wanted to rip the picture from her grasp and tear it into a thousand pieces, it looked that much like him.

When I finally got on the force, I took a copy of the picture from the database. I keep it in my desk drawer as a reminder—he's still out there…I just have to find him.

"Mrs. Stevens," I start as I loosen the grip on the neatly folded image in my hand, and thrust it her way, "does this man look familiar to you?"

Taking it from me, she carefully opens it and her eyes narrow as she inspects it. For a moment, I want to say recognition flickers in her eyes, but after a long minute, she shakes her head and hands it back.

"I don't know this man."

I make the mistake of glancing down at the image and his soulless dark eyes glare at me in warning. *I'm coming for you, pretty little doll.* A shudder passes through me and I swallow down my terror. "Can you tell me about the last time you saw your daughter?"

"We argued," she chokes, losing her composure. I hand her a tissue and urge her on.

She shakes her head and shrugs. "It was nothing really, just about her taking money from my purse without asking."

Sniffling, she swipes the tissue across her nose, catches a fallen drip, and smiles over at me, embarrassed.

"She just started her period. Didn't tell me about it though and took money to buy tampons. I'm an understanding momma. I know what it's like. If she just told me in the first place..." she sobs, sucking in a gulp of air. "I'm a woman and girls need their mommas for these things. I would have taken her to get them." She stares at me with red, teary eyes, waiting for...what? Understanding?

I could offer none.

My cell is freezing at night and I'm regretting butchering Benny's doll. My meltdown achieved nothing except leaving me half-naked and embarrassed.

And cold.

So cold.

I hate being exposed in only my bra and panties. Spiders keep skittering across the dusty floor and finding their way to my legs to bite me, leaving my skin hypersensitive and itchy.

I want to call out to Macy, but he doesn't let us talk when he's here. When he goes off for a day or two, we talk. Though, she doesn't say much anymore and I have to coax conversation from her. I'm not sure how long we've been here exactly. Weeks? Months? It's hard to tell.

My stomach cramps and I rub my hand over the chilled flesh to ease it. It's been doing that a lot over the past few days. What if I'm dying? Flicking my gaze to the makeshift toilet in the corner of my cell, I cringe. I hate using that filthy thing and it hurts my legs to hover over it.

I lift from the bed and start to walk over to the toilet when a dampness coats between my legs. My hand drops to touch the wetness and my eyes grow wide when it comes back smeared in blood.

Looking down, I find my white panties soaked in a cerise patch.

I'm bleeding.

My chest quakes and a silent sob aches my ribcage.

"What is that?"

A gasp escapes my lips at his voice. I thought he would be sleeping on the cot he has beside his work table just outside our cells, but he's not. He's peering in at me, staring at the blood staining my panties and inner thighs.

"My period," I mutter, afraid and humiliated. The door lock clanks and then swings open. Highlighted by a lamplight glowing by his cot, his muscles tense and sweat sticks to his skin like a fine mist. He's beautiful and it's haunting.

I hate him.

As he takes a step toward me, I take a step back, and his eyes narrow at my retreating movements.

My hands attempt to hide my panty-covered private parts, trying to conceal my shame from him.

He already takes enough from me; my dignity is still mine.

With a grumble, he swipes at me, effortlessly knocking my hands away. His frame crowds my smaller one and then his hands brush over my hips, making my body tremble and erupt in goosebumps.

Don't touch me, don't touch me, don't touch me, *I scream over and over in my head, but terror keeps me mute.*

Tucking his thumbs into the waist of my panties, he drags them down my legs. "Step out," he commands, and I swallow the lump forming in my throat.

He's on one knee in front of me, his breath, hot and intrusive, on my lower stomach.

"You stink," he announces.

Shame and horror threatens to consume me.

"Dirty little doll." His fingers stroke at the blood painting the skin of my thigh. When he slips the fingers into his mouth to taste the blood and then pulls them out with a vulgar pop, I gag.

"You're a woman now," he announces. Before I can speak, he stands and marches from my cell, taking my spoiled underwear with him.

When he gets outside the door, he stops and glares back at me. "Don't. Fucking. Move."

My legs twitch, instinct telling me to run. A war rages between my head and the adrenaline building in my bloodstream.

You won't make it.

Run.

He will catch you.

Run.

Macy.

I stumble forward slightly, but it's unnoticeable to him as he returns to my cell with a bucket. Soapy water splashes around as he carries it over to me and drops back to his knees. He picks up a sponge and wrings it out, the scent of apple assaulting my nose. The warmth of the sponge against my humming flesh is the best thing I've felt since he stole me.

"I can do it myself," I murmur, my voice hoarse and wary.

"No," he says, a low growl escaping him. "I will clean my dirty little doll." He dips the sponge back into the water and taps my leg with the other hand.

When I don't move, he taps it again, harder.

Squeezing my thighs together, I refuse his voiceless command.

Smacking my skin once more, causing a sting, he attempts to get me to spread them apart. I grit my teeth and remain defiant.

"Stay dirty then," he snaps before getting to his feet and taking the bucket with him, but I don't want to be dirty and sticky. I reach for his arm in a bout of desperation.

"No, please."

He looks down at my hand on his arm and I quickly yank it back.

I part my legs to show him I'll do as I'm told and he watches me for a moment, studying me in silence. Without warning, a force of water collides against the apex of my thighs with a whoosh, making me gasp.

He cleans me quickly and efficiently, and then he's gone and the cell door is clanking shut. I'm about to break down at the thought of being without panties when his arm dangles through the bars, blocking out the soft orange glow, a pair of pink panties hanging from his finger.

"Detective?"

I jerk my gaze from the picture and find Mrs. Stevens' questioning eyes.

A sheen of sweat has soaked my shirt from the inside out.

"I'm sorry…"

She frowns. "Is this the man you think took my daughter? Do you know this man? Oh God, is he a serial killer?"

Backtracking, I scramble to calm her. "No, I'm just following all leads."

Her head shakes as she points at me. "You know him. Whoever this is. You're crying, Detective."

My mouth parts open and I swipe away the rogue tears that gave me away. "I, uh…he's just someone…"

"What did he do? Dear God," she chokes out.

Frowning, I lean forward and take her hand.

"This man hurt me and my sister a very long time ago. But I have reason to believe he's out there again. It may have nothing to do with your daughter, but I can assure you I won't sleep until I find her. I'm personally invested in this case."

And that's why I shouldn't be here. I'm risking my badge, divulging this stuff to her, losing my shit, and letting my memories steal me from the present.

Tears spill down over her cheeks and she squeezes my hand.

"Don't let him hurt my baby girl. Oh God, please."

"I won't allow it, I promise," I say, trying to comfort her, but it's false promises. What if he already has hurt her?

"Thank you," she chokes. "Thank you. I'm so sorry for whatever happened to you."

Giving her a deceptive smile, I stand and nod. "Me too."

"You gonna tell me what happened earlier today?" Dillon questions, his eyes on mine as he stirs way too much sugar into his coffee.

The man will have diabetes by the time he's forty if

he's not careful. "It won't make you sweeter." I gesture to the sugar and he grins.

"You think I'm sweet enough?"

I snort. "Not what I meant."

He nods his head and tilts it to the side "I know what you are trying to do. Not happening. Now, answer the question."

"It was nothing." My lie causes his brows to lift. There's nothing getting past this guy.

"You flipping your shit is hardly nothing. I've been watching you for eight months and you've never lost it like that," he says, his voice dropping a few octaves. "Something happened and we're not leaving this coffee shop until you tell me what it was."

"Watching me for eight months?" I query, humming birds vibrating in my stomach, though I don't know why. Lowering his head, he coughs and pats his chest

"Working with you for eight months—working, not watching. You're trying to stray from the topic at hand," he accuses, not looking me in the eye.

My gaze falls to the napkin I've been shredding. "It won't happen again," I tell him, my voice firm.

Our eyes meet again. In the warm sunlight pouring in through the window, his are a molten chocolate brown. I've never noticed just how long his dark lashes are either. Dillon is handsome. I've seen the way the women at the station fall all over themselves to talk to him, but to be honest with myself, I've never paid too much attention. *Liar.*

He's always treated me like a burden and I've responded in kind. Now that he's showing concern, I see him in a literal new light—and it irks me. I don't want our dynamic to change. I can't handle him caring and wanting to get inside my thoughts. He won't like it in there.

Dirty little doll.

He brings his mug to his full lips and sips on the hot liquid, never breaking our gaze. A five o'clock shadow dusts his cheeks, and it looks good on him. When he sets his mug back down, he runs his fingers through his overgrown dark hair and pins me with a stare that says *we can sit here all day.*

Understanding I'm not getting off that easy, I let out a resigned huff.

"You've read my file or know of it."

A flash of anger passes over his features and he gives me a clipped nod. "Psycho."

Benny or *me*?

"Ya think?" I bark out with a harsh laugh.

He takes another sip of his coffee, his dark brows furling together. I've never had his undivided attention and quite frankly, it unnerves me. I'm hyperaware of the messy bun I pulled my hair into this morning. Of the way my button-down shirt is undone one more from the top than usual to allow the cool air to kiss my flesh. Of the way I'd hastily slapped on makeup before walking out the door, not taking too much time to look pretty.

Pretty little doll.

A shudder ripples through me and he slaps the table, startling me.

"There, Jade. Right there. Talk." His tone leaves no room for argument.

"I, uh…I freaked because…" I trail off and blink away

the tears fighting for release. "The dolls. My abductor used to make dolls. He even sold them at the flea market. It's how he lured us into his van that day."

Dillon doesn't speak, but his jaw ticks as he clenches his teeth and those molten chocolate eyes flare with fury, causing amber licks to spark that weren't apparent earlier.

"I saw the dolls and I was there. I was back in the cell with him. His body was..." I choke on my words, "His breath...oh, Jesus."

"Sick fuck," Dillon growls.

Benny or *me*?

The screech of the door closing behind him startles me awake. My cell is pitch black and he doesn't turn on any lights to break the darkness hovering in the dead of night, but I can feel his presence. Deep, ragged breaths echo around me. Sitting up on the mattress, I squint, trying to adjust my eyes through the inky veil.

"What do you want from me?" I hiss, careful not to wake my sister.

He sits on the bed beside me, his heat scorching the air between us, and I cower away from him. When his hand snatches my bicep and hauls me to him, I cry out despite wanting to be quiet.

He had just killed another girl. I didn't watch this time, but their faces are phantoms in my head, their screams echo in my dreamless mind at night.

She wasn't right, *he'd chanted while butchering her. I couldn't block out her screams and gurgles as she drowned in her own life essence.*

Four girls had come and left via the spirit world and my inner voice always asked why he kept us.

But he did.

He kept us locked away.

Apart from each other and lonely for affection.

Starved of comfort and connections.

"She wasn't right. Not pretty enough close up and she lied. Why do they lie about their age? She wasn't twenty-one, her license said nineteen. Why lie?" he asks me, but I don't think he wants an answer. He never has in the past.

His hands vibrate as he rubs them down his jean clad thighs. He's shirtless, like normal, and blood clings to his skin, making him look like a wicked piece of art.

"Why do you keep us?" I find the words leaving my mouth before I can think. My sleepy state has left me bold.

When his head turns to look down at me, I gulp and try not to wilt under his gaze.

"You," he says simply.

"Me?"

"I keep you." His hand cups my cheek and my chest restricts me from inhaling air.

His body surrounds mine, sucking the oxygen from the room, from my lungs.

This is new.

"You're the prettiest doll I've ever seen." His breath hits my face with a puff of heat.

Pretty?

He usually calls me the dirty doll.

Never pretty.

My skin crawls when his mouth comes closer and he inhales the space between my ear and shoulder. It tickles *when he sighs and nuzzles against my hair. I'm used to his abuse. His cruel words. His starvation torture techniques.*

I'm used to hearing him go on and on about how much he loves to dress my sister in ridiculous dresses and how he paints her face like she's a real life doll. I'm used to the way he bathes us with a rag and rubs our flesh raw.

For three years, this has been our life.

Us being his prisoners in a world that only makes sense to him.

I'm not used to this.

His gentle touch.

The eager crackle of energy in the air.

I'm terrified.

Just as I've changed and grown into a woman over the years, he too has changed.

He's taller and his muscles bigger. The cut in his abs and the deep indents on his hips are more defined and prudent. His hair is longer and untamed for months at a time.

"I want to play with my dirty little doll. I can't wait any longer. Do you feel ready—old enough?" he pleads into my neck, his hands balling into fists at either side of my head.

No…

"Don't," I manage to choke out.

He rises above me, piercing me with his hollow eyes.

"I want to play with my dirty little doll." His repeated words send a shiver of fear rippling through me. "You are mine. All mine. I'm not waiting anymore."

His tongue darts out and tastes my neck just below my ear. I'm frozen—too afraid to move. When his hand slides down the front of my bare chest and clutches onto my breast, the world spins around me.

I'd outgrown my bra forever ago, the one I had when I arrived here.

Arrived...like a hotel guest.

When I defied him one time by refusing to take it off so he could wash me, he tore it and my panties from me and made me live naked ever since.

"It's time for me to love my dirty doll." He strokes his hand over my face. "So damn pretty, perfect, this face." His eyes swoop over me. "This body." His knee jerks between my legs, forcing them to part. "Your precious, pure cunt."

Vomit burns in my throat and hot lava gushes from my eyes, burning my cheeks in the process.

Wiggling beneath him in the hopeless act of trying to shake him off is met with resistance as his weight pins me to the bed.

Hands splay and grope at me. The copper scent of blood from the slain dolly fills my nose. He shuffles on top of me, his feet tugging at the legs of his jeans, making them shift down his waist until his hot, hard length slaps against my stomach.

I shake my head no as realization of what's to come washes over me like a cold rain.

"Don't, please."

"I'm loving you," he hisses, placing a hand over my mouth to silence me.

Love.

What a stupid word coming out of his hateful mouth.

The only love I've ever felt was that of my sister and parents. Certainly not Benny. I'll never feel love for this evil monster taking more of me than he already has. There will be nothing left.

He lifts my leg over his arm, spreading me open. The prod of his member stabs at me until he reaches between our bodies and lines it up at my entrance.

My eyes bulge as he shoves into me. I squeeze them shut, fire exploding behind my lids as I hold my breath and will the excruciating pain to subside.

Why does it hurt so bad? Why would people choose to do this?

His weight is still crushing me. His breathing is deep and tense.

"Perfect," he announces.

I want to tear at his flesh until he's nothing but pulp.

"It will only hurt for a minute," he assures me before thrusting into me over and over again.

He lied.

It doesn't ever stop hurting.

When he finally ceases moving and grunts, hot liquid empties inside me and spills out. It stings like crazy and I want to wipe it away, but I'm frozen to the bed. I'll never get this back.

His weight lifts from mine to sit next to me. He rubs over his cock and with the pad of his thumb, he coats my lips in the residue of my innocence, like it's lipstick.

"My pretty, perfect, dirty little doll." His head drops toward me and his lips hover over mine. "There's no one like you."

And then he's gone and I'm alone, empty and dying inside.

Ruined.

Slamming my eyes shut, I attempt to think of happier things, but come up short.

I don't know what the hell makes me happy.

Macy.

Macy.

Macy.

When a strong arm wraps around me, I let out a shriek. It's only then I realize Dillon has slipped into the booth beside me and hauled me against his solid body. A tear sneaks its way out, much to my dismay, but I don't push him away or joke off my distress.

I obligingly let him hold me. It's surreal to feel the tears on my cheek knowing they're soaking against the cotton of his shirt and he doesn't judge me in this moment. I haven't cried in so long.

His large hand strokes up and down the side of my arm, soothing my rapidly beating heart. The scent of peppermint and leather, now mixed with coffee, calms me and I relax in his grip. It's easier than I ever imagined it would be. I fit against him like the curve of his body was created for this moment—created to shield a sorrow-filled woman from being buried in the memories of a broken little girl. Sighing into his body, I relish the comfort, grateful to him for not being his usual mocking self.

After a moment, he speaks. With my head against him, I can feel the deep rumble rattle its way through me. "The doll. In the shop," he says, his voice gravelly, "was it familiar?"

"Yes."

"You think the homicide may be tied to your own cold case?"

I nod and chew on my bottom lip. "And the girl who was taken from the mall. A witness claims she saw her speaking with someone who matches Benny's description. It all ties together, Dillon. I swear, I'm not crazy."

Lifting my head, I look into his eyes to see if he believes me. Huge mistake. With my emotions all over the place and the monster from my past fresh in my thoughts, I suddenly find myself greedy for more of Dillon's comfort. A shameful thought enters my mind and I quickly shove it away. But when his dark eyes skim to my lips for a brief moment, heat floods through me.

"You're not so much of a bitch from this angle," he teases before releasing me. "But you're still annoying." He winks and returns to his side of the table, and my skin instantly chills at the loss of him.

Thoughts of Bo creep into my conscience and I want to throw up.

I'm a terrible person.

This is exactly why I shouldn't marry him.

"I'm engaged," I blurt out.

Apparently, I just don't know when to quit.

A look I can't quite interpret flashes over his face before he clears his throat. "Congratu-fucking-lations." He forces a grin. "Now, tell me about this asshole and how we're going to finally nab him."

I think about the moments just before now, when I was reliving Benny stealing my virginity.

That was the gentlest he had ever been with me. After that first time, he became greedy for my body and his monster let off its leash was ruthless. He liked to constantly tell me how he wasn't a pervert and my body was fully developed—he was obsessed with convincing not just me, but I think himself. His issues ran deep.

Dillon wants to know about that asshole. Just like Bo wanted to know all the details about him.

But they can't handle the reality of what happened to me.

Hell, I can barely handle it.

I cower as I remember what Benny made of me in the end. If they knew everything about him, then they'd learn everything about me.

Shame drenches me.

They can't know.

"Please..." My plea fades into a whisper when his hand continues to travel south, "I'm on my period."

He chuckles and the vibrations shake my very soul. "I know. You've been leaking down your thighs all week. But you're nearly done bleeding, dirty little doll."

"I don't want—" My words die in my throat the moment he touches me between my legs. I squirm to get away, but he rubs me in a place that jolts electricity through me.

He knew my body better than I did now, and at times, it didn't even feel like my own. It was like my own body was betraying me and craved to feel the release he offered. It's my only escape out of this place.

"Lie back and let me love you," he murmurs, his fingers massaging circles below the thatch of my pubic hair. With each swirl of his strong fingers, I get swept up into this sick nightmare further and further.

Pleasure pulsates through me, numbing my cuts and

bruises from an outburst he had earlier when I called his latest porcelain doll ugly.

Foreign sensations still the constant roar of hate inside my head. I'm caught up in his wicked web, left for him to devour in some way I can't even comprehend or anticipate.

Before I even realize it, I'm lying on my back on the mattress. My thighs have fallen apart as he continues his assault on me, and I don't fight it off one bit.

I'm usually the fighter.

I normally claw at him and hiss and scream when he hurts me.

But he's done something to my mind by being gentle, by transitioning what we shared before to this new thing he does with my body.

He finally broke me.

And I'm letting him do things I never knew were possible.

"Oh..." I whine, every muscle in my body tightening with the need for release.

Release of what?

"That's it, pretty little doll. Show me you love me."

Tears well in my eyes. I'm weak—so darn weak for not pushing him away. I should kick him in the face. Run while I can. Yet, I don't. It's futile anyway. He's too strong,

"Oh!"

"Relax," he states, "let it happen."

And then it does.

Whatever it is.

Blinding white light explodes around me in my pitch black cell. A pleasure I never knew existed possesses my body until I'm shuddering without abandon. Nothing makes sense. Benny hurts me. And now he touches me in ways that feel good.

I'm lost in my thoughts when his heavy body falls over mine, crushing me beneath him.

I can feel his…

"Oh God," I moan when the tip of his penis pushes against my slick opening.

I start to cry out in disgust of myself. I have mixed reactions and emotions, my mind telling me one thing, but my body saying another. Human contact in any form after a while becomes longed for.

His mouth on mine silences me. He's never put his mouth on mine. He's never kissed me on the lips.

What's happening?

"Shhh," he murmurs, hot breath tickling my lips as he begins pushing his thickness deep inside me.

He doesn't normally care if he hurts me.

He loves to hurt me.

I don't understand.

I sob as the pain of letting him bring such pleasures conflicts me. His thrusts increase and he begins pounding away, getting rougher, plowing into me so hard, my body jolts and shifts beneath him. It feels as though he's ripping me in two. And for all I know, maybe he is. Maybe he's going to rip me apart and consume the remnants of my soul.

"Shhh, I love you, pretty little doll."

Sobs choke my throat as tears streak down my cheeks, causing me to hyperventilate. It's official. I'm in hell. He remains still inside me while I attempt to catch my breath.

"You're mine. All mine. Love me, my pretty little doll," he murmurs, his lips finding my neck. He suckles my flesh *and begins kissing me in an almost reverent way that confuses me. I'm so caught up in his kisses, I don't realize he's also massaging just above where he's inside me. Curls of pleasure begin to build again and the pain of him within me subsides.*

And I need...

I lie there, my hands fisted at my sides, but as he makes me feel good again, the urge to touch him takes over.

Contact. Connection.

My fingers skitter up his sculpted shoulders as a fantasy begins playing in my mind.

That he loves us now.

He'll be kind.

He'll let us go.

He's changing. This will all be over soon.

The thought is fleeting. He will never let his dolls go.

His lips find mine again and he kisses me with an emotion I feel down to my very being. He believes this is love. That this is real.

It's not.

But if I play along, maybe he'll take me out of my cell.

I could see Macy...

We could get away.

I slide my fingers into his hair and kiss him back with a fervor I didn't know I possessed. He bucks into me and it hurts, but if I let him believe he's claiming me down to a cellular level, then maybe he really will fall and want to be with me outside these walls. His body consumes mine and I get lost in the role I'm playing.

The pleasure overrules the pain, distracting me to the point that I'm a willing participant, pretend or not.

My fingers grip at his long, curly hair and I spread my legs as far apart as they'll go.

He drives into me powerfully—reminding me once again he's a man and I'm just his doll. But the way he whispers kisses over my lips as though I am precious to him makes me think I'm succeeding in making him love me for real. Perhaps I'm growing powerful too. Do breasts and body hair and periods play tricks on men? Am I turning into his woman in his eyes?

"Fuck, you're so perfect," he grunts, nipping at my lip, biting down and drawing blood. It's his way of being playful, loving even. He likes to paint my lips red with blood.

The sound of his skin slapping mine makes my flesh heat. A building within me starts pulsing like before, but more powerful. I need the sensation again like I need to breathe. "Do you love me?"

His words startle me, but his fingers never stop moving between my legs. He never slows his thrusting. Those lips I hate never stop kissing me.

No!

"Y-Yes," I stammer.

I hate you!

He groans. "I'm going to come."

That means he'll be finished soon. I'm trying to plan my escape when pleasure sears through me once again—hot, white, wicked. It triggers a response within him too. His penis seems to double in size, then a rush of hot liquid pours into me.

My body is mush. I'm nothing but a rag doll—his rag doll.

He slips out of me and the heat runs down my butt

crack to the mattress below me. I lie there unmoving as he shuffles about. I've dazed out for who knows how long and don't come to until I feel a warm, wet cloth between my legs.

"You're so dirty, little doll."

For once, his words don't make me shudder. I let him cleanse me and don't fight him. My mind is scrambled and confused, but it's the first time he's come into my cell where I've felt like I had some power back.

It's the first time he's done anything nice.

What if he does these things to Macy?

The thought seizes my lungs and I choke out my words. "D-Do you do this with my sister?"

His chuckle is warm in the dark room. It doesn't chill me like usual. It creates an inner burning that didn't exist before.

"Do you want me to?"

No. Please...no.

I shake my head hard.

His hand grips my chin and his gaze delves into my own, hunting past the layers of defense to get to the vulnerability beneath.

"Just you, dirty little doll," he assures me. "It's just you."

The memory of Benny is too fresh. My heart pounds in my chest and it's almost as if I can still feel the disgusting throb he used to evoke from me between my thighs. Benny fucked me up in the head and turned my body against me more times than I can remember. All these years later, and he still finds me. He still knows how to make my thoughts betray me.

I may not be in that cell anymore, but Benny is every bit still my master.

CHAPTER FIVE

~ *Carmine* ~

"Scott. Phillips. My office. Now!" Chief Stanton's voice roars from down the hall.

My eyes lift from my report, meeting Dillon's confused stare. He gives me a clipped nod before standing. Normally he'd be busting my balls, trying to rile me up, but something changed after this afternoon in the coffee shop.

We became partners.

Two people dedicated to solve an important case together.

An unstoppable duo.

Friends?

When I stand and pass him, his palm presses into my lower back just above my ass as he guides us down the hallway. And dammit if I don't shiver at his touch while my flesh heats where his hand rests. I attempt to push away wrong thoughts and focus on whatever shit-show we're about to walk into.

As we reach the office, Dillon drops his hand and stalks off ahead of me. Stanton is standing beside the door, red-faced and heaving angry breaths.

What the hell did we do now?

Once inside, he slams the door so hard, I let out a squeak of surprise. Dillon growls and stands between Chief and me, as if to shield me from his rage. As much as that warms me, it'll only piss our boss off even more. I touch Dillon's arm softly before finding my seat. He follows after me.

"I want to know why you two thought it was okay to go against direct orders," Stanton seethes as he lurches himself into his chair. He leans forward, elbows on his desk, and glares at me in particular.

"I don't know what you mean—" I start, but he cuts me off with a slam of his fist to the desk.

"Bullshit!"

"Okay, Chief, you need to calm down," Dillon barks.

But Stanton is far from calm. He's enraged. I've pissed him off a lot, sure, but I have never seen him this out of control before.

"Alena Stevens. Missing girl. I told Lieutenant Wallis to have you two reassigned. You were to work the homicide at the doll shop. Why in the ever-loving hell would you continue to pursue the missing person case?"

Dillon jerks his head to me and frowns. I shake my head, rolling my eyes, my stare meeting that of Stanton's. "I know, but I was in the neighborhood and thought the cases might be related. Turns out, they are."

Chief's face turns so red, I think he might explode. "Do you have any idea what sort of media catastrophe you caused, Phillips?"

I dart my gaze to Dillon and he's just as perplexed. "I don't know what you mean, sir."

"Oh, don't try the sir bullshit on me now, Detective."

He grips his computer monitor and drags it around for us to view. "You told that woman whoever took her daughter was the same person who took you all those years ago!"

"No!" I argue, my entire body tensing. "I told her maybe. That it was possible."

"Not what the media claims," he snarls.

It's then I read the headline on one of our local news stations.

Cold Case is on Fire as Police Link Alena Stevens to Missing Girls from Twelve Years Ago.

I close my eyes and attempt to burn away the image of Alena's face next to mine and my sister's. Swallowing, I blink my eyes back open and look at Stanton. "I can explain. They have to be related. You see, the doll from the window—"

He barks out a laugh and slams his hand on his desk, making me jerk from the impact. "They found the girl."

They found the girl.

Sickness stirs in my stomach.

"Are you sure you want to see these?" Dad asks me, plonking a box on the table before us with a thud.

Our eyes meet and my gaze is firm. "Just show me."

After lifting the lid, he nudges the box toward me. Mom reaches across from her chair next to me and squeezes my hand.

I've been home a week. Just one week. My old room was unchanged, left exactly as it was four years ago, just like Macy's.

It was familiar, but strange. Comforting, but agonizing.

Only part of me had returned, the other part was still there in that cell with my sister. My parents have been overjoyed at having me back, but I can see the way their eyes meet when I'm not looking. The questions dancing there on the tips of their tongues. The wondering about what happened to their two little girls. The unfairness that they'd only been given one daughter back instead of two.

The burning question in my own head: do they blame me?

I blame me.

With a loud exhaled sigh, I pick up the first newspaper cutting and my body tenses.

Sisters Still Missing—Community Fears for their Safety as Hunt Continues.

Macy smiles back at me from the image of her—so young and fresh faced.

She's thirteen now. Four whole years had passed with us locked away, yet life went on.

Bo next door graduated college. The neighbors finally finished the extension on their house. Mom still worked at the diner and Dad at the garage.

Life went on…without us.

I drop the page and pick up another.

Body of Missing Teen Emma Miles Discovered

The slain body of missing teen Emma Miles was discovered in the early hours of yesterday morning detectives confirm.

Emma Miles went missing three days ago from a carnival where she was enjoying a night out with friends.

It hasn't been determined if this case is related to that of missing locals, Jade and Macy Phillips, who disappeared over a year ago and have yet to be found.

My hand shakes as the innocent eyes of the girl who lives inside me stares up at the shell of a person I've become. The memory of him smashing her face into the mirror is still vivid in my mind despite the time that's passed.

"How many, Mom?"

She doesn't need to ask what I'm referring to. She can sense it in my sorrowful tone.

"Four in total, but older. They didn't know if they were related to your case. There were four girls until a year ago, and then none. The case went cold." Her tone is tired as she flicks her weary gaze to me. She's aged in the time I've been gone. Lines mar her forehead and crinkle her eyes.

I counted four too, and then there were no more, not since the night he took my virginity.

Would he start again now that I was gone?

I knock the box to the floor as I stumble to my feet and rush to the bathroom. Vomit spurts out of me and when my stomach is finally empty, I cry over the toilet bowl, wishing I could be washed away with the flush.

"Where?" Dillon shouts, jerking me from my past. "Where was she found?"

I blink away my daze and focus on Chief's words.

"Alena Stevens went off with a boy she met at the mall. But after a day with this boy and realizing he wasn't all he was cracked up to be, she came home." His cold gaze finds mine.

A gasp leaves me in a rush. "He let her go? Benny let her go?"

Dillon places his palm on my knee to keep it from bouncing. "Just stop, Jade."

I blink in confusion and my eyes dart back to Stanton. "I don't understand. They're related. I know these two cases are related!"

My partner squeezes my thigh to get me to shut up, but I can't. Nothing makes sense. I just knew he'd taken the girl. Just like he'd taken me. He was back. Hunting for more dolls.

"I want your badge and gun. Not only are you off the homicide case," Chief snaps, "you're taking some administrative leave. I don't want to see you until all this shit blows over. You made the whole department look like a bunch of incompetent fools letting a victimized woman trample all over both cases. Your ass is gone for the rest of the week."

I remain still as a statue as his words wash over me.

Unrelated cases.

Off the case.

Administrative leave.

"But, Chief..."

Dillon taps my thigh and shakes his head sadly at me. "Come on, I'll walk you out."

Once we're outside, the wind whips at my flesh and I welcome its icy lashing. "I could have sworn it was him," I whisper, dropping my head in shame. With a firm grip, he drags me by the arm into his chest and I let him, collapsing against his body. His comforting me is a new revelation in our friendship but I can't lie and say I don't like it. I like it too much pressed up against his solid chest. Dillon's warmth envelops me and I feel safe. For once in my life, I relax and let someone truly hold me. It's the most peace I've felt in a long time.

He only keeps me there for a brief moment before pushing me toward my car. "Get the fuck out of here. Chief only did this to get you to take some time off for once." He smiles to reassure me, but it doesn't work. "And don't think I've forgotten you still owe me a hundred bucks," he teases in an attempt to lighten the mood, and I flip him off.

"Thank you for everything," I murmur, almost inaudible, as I open my car door and slide into the seat.

He grabs the door before I can pull it closed. "We'll get him eventually, Jade. They always fuck up, and when he does, I promise we'll get him."

I stare into the now empty tumbler and rattle it. When Bo gets home, I'm going to have to break the news to him. I fucked up. The very idea of confessing how my awful day had gone has bile rising in my throat.

I'd been so sure.

I'm still wallowing in my failure when I hear the front door open. My fiancé is noisy as he comes inside, his keys jangling along the way.

"Babe?"

He walks into the kitchen to see me sitting on the island, my legs dangling off the counter with a half-empty bottle of whiskey at my side. His eyes widen for a brief moment before he chucks his keys onto the counter and stalks over to me.

"Jesus, Jade," he murmurs as he wraps his arms around me. "What happened?"

Emotion makes my throat ache. "Everything."

He pulls me off the counter to my unstable feet. When I sway, he hugs me to him. His lips find the top of my head and he peppers kisses on my hair, attempting to soothe me. Thing is, I'm not feeling very soothed. Not at all like how Dillon had a funny way of calming me earlier today in the middle of my mental breakdown.

A shudder courses through me.

I'm doing it again.

Obsessing over Dillon's newfound human appeal when I need to be present with my…fiancé. Another shiver passes through me.

"Come on," he mutters. "Let's get you to bed."

He somehow wrangles me into the bedroom and begins peeling off my clothes. Bo is such a good man—so caring and protective. He'll make a good husband one day.

To someone else.

The thought makes me feel sick inside.

He doesn't want someone else, though. He wants me. I need to make myself want him too. As soon as he frees me of my jeans and I'm left in nothing but my panties, I attack him. A low, satisfied growl rumbles through him as I grip his hardening cock through his slacks.

"Fuck me, Bo."

Our teeth clash together as he rips his clothes off in record time. He'll lay me on the bed and be inside me by my next breath. He'll whisper sweet nothings as he makes love to me. Sweet Bo is so predictable.

Just once I'd like for him to lose control and actually

fuck me.

Like him?

My brain shuts down as I remember the first time I was fucked.

"On your stomach."

His barked order startles me and I flinch, frowning at him in confusion. "Why?"

I'm worried he'll go back to hurting me. For months now, he's done these things to my body. He's made me feel pleasure I was still too young to really know about. The very idea of him coming in here while in his darkened monster state makes me almost hysterical.

"Don't question me," he roars, "just do it."

I scramble to heed his instruction at the dead tone of his warning. He's naked and has never come to me like this before. It's usually in the dead of night when he's calm.

I'm still hopeful he'll want me to love him.

I'll never love him.

That he'll call me his pretty little doll.

That he'll put his mouth between my legs like he's recently started doing and make my mind leave my cell for a brief moment.

"Such a pretty little doll," he murmurs.

I relax at his words.

He slaps my butt with his palm, leaving a burn there and then he squeezes one cheek with such brutality it winds me.

He rustles with the other hand for something in his pocket, then drops a piece of paper at my face. Gripping my hair in a fist, he raises my head and makes me stare down at the image.

It's a newspaper article about the anniversary of my and Macy's disappearance. In the image is an old picture my daddy took. It's of me and Macy. Bo from next door is butted up against me with an arm slung over my shoulder and his dog Toby lying at our feet as we lean against Dad's flatbed truck.

"Who is this?" *he seethes, his tone so deadly, the chill from it creeps into my bones and freezes me.*

"No one," *I assure him, my voice a whisper.* "Just my neighbor."

"Then why in the hell is his arm around you like you belong to him?" *he snarls possessively, and I wither in fright.* "I'm going to fuck you. You're mine, little doll. Not his. Mine."

I'm about to question what the difference between lovemaking and fucking is when he keeps hold of my hair, yanking my head back even farther, stretching me so much, it restricts my breathing.

"Ahhh!" *I wheeze out past trembling lips.*

"Beg for it! Tell me whose dolly you are!"

Tears streak down my cheeks as I struggle to put my hands on the mattress to keep my hair from being pulled right from my scalp. "Please!"

"Please what?" *he demands as he shoves apart my thighs with his knee.*

"I'm your doll…"

His grip loosens and I fall back against the new pillow he recently gifted me. People take pillows for granted until they go without one for three years. And when you are gifted one, you'll feel such appreciation, you almost forget the monster lurking within him.

I yelp when he pushes his hardened cock inside my hot center. As always, my body is receptive and accepting for him.

He's all I've known. The only contact I have.

He oftentimes makes me go without food, feeding my body with his "love" instead.

More times than not, I forgo food anyway, just to have that delicious feeling of my body floating my thoughts away from me.

"You're my little doll," *he groans against my hair as he thrusts brutally into me. I'm not used to him taking me this way. Everything feels more intense.*

"Yes."

"I want to choke the shit out of my little dolly."

Tears well in my eyes and I start to argue, but his palm wraps around my throat. His grip is tight and unyielding as he pounds into me from behind. I'm powerless to pull him off me as I struggle to breathe. His whole weight crushes me, but he somehow manages to slide a palm around to my stomach, pulling me closer to him.

Will he kill me like the other dolls?

The thought terrifies me, but not like it should. I don't want Macy to be alone.

For him to do this to her.

To be disposable to him.

The air thickens around me and I'm aware of the darkness cloaking my senses, smothering me. I'm blacking out with this thought on my mind, but the moment he touches my clit, he revives me. Like the confused girl I am, I choose an orgasm over air—just like I choose them over nourish-

ment.

"Good girl," he mutters, his grip loosening slightly. "Love me."

I suck tiny hisses of air into my lungs, but it isn't what I'm greedy for. I'm greedy for the intense pleasure I know he'll gift me if I simply hold still. He continues his relentless thrusting while his fingers do their magical dance.

Between his expert touches and the brutal way he takes me with his massive hand around my throat, I release harder than I ever have before. I completely black out with his whispered name, the name he won't allow us to say, on my lips.

Benny.
Benny.

"Benny."

The movement stops and I blink my eyes open as Bo's beautiful face crumples in devastation.

"Were you…" his voice drops to a whisper, "were you thinking about that monster?"

God, no.

Yes.

My lip wobbles. This seems like a terrible time to discuss this—with him balls deep inside my vagina. "I, uh…I had a terrible day."

He slips out of me and jumps out of the bed as if I'm a snake that's just bitten him. "What happened?"

I frown as he dresses with record speed. "Chief put me on leave. I thought the missing girl and today's homicide were related to…"

"Related to what?" he snaps.

"Benny."

His lip curls in anger. My sweet Bo doesn't look sweet at all. He looks pissed. "This shit again, Jade? Not every missing girl or homicide is that sick fucking prick."

This shit?

Did he just expect me to let it go?

Does he not see Benny lives inside me, still keeping me prisoner in my mind?

"I want you to go back to your therapist," he hisses, a cold bite in his voice. "You've gotten worse lately. It's making you crazy, Jade."

At this, I sit up on my elbows and glare. "You know how I feel about the therapist. It doesn't help. It only makes things worse. We talk in circles and nothing gets solved. I'm not going back. I made a mistake and I have a week to think it over."

He scrubs his face with his palm. "Why didn't you wear your ring?"

Guilt slides over me like oil on a lake. "My job—"

"You're lying. Did you even tell anyone about our engagement? Your parents?"

I close my eyes.

"I told my partner," I push out.

A harsh laugh escapes him. "Babe, you need to get your shit together. I've stood by idly for long enough, but I won't watch you destroy yourself from the inside out. See the therapist or..." he trails off, his gaze hardening.

"Or what?"

"Forget it." He stomps off into the closet.

Scrambling out of the bed on clumsy, still-drunk feet,

I charge after him. "Or what, Bo?"

He shoves some clothes into a backpack and the hangers clang together as each shirt comes loose. "Or we may as well throw in the towel now. How the fuck are we going to bring kids into a situation like this?"

Kids?

I gape at him with a dumfounded look on my face.

"Like I said," he huffs, "forget it. I always knew it would be hard getting you on the same page as me. I just didn't know it would be fucking impossible."

A tear streaks down my cheek as he pushes past me out of the closet.

"Where are you going?"

He shrugs. "I'm going to Mom's. If you need me, you can find me there. You apparently need some space to get your head together. I'll be waiting for you when you snap out of it. Like usual."

Don't go. Don't leave me alone.

I stand there naked, my mouth open in shock as I watch the boy who has always been there for me walk out the door.

CHAPTER SIX

~ Indian Red ~

Looking around the apartment this woman, or doctor...or whatever she is, calls an office, I see a thousand items no one person could possibly need in their lifetime. So many...things.

There are no photos or evidence of a family.

Just her things.

As if she collects them to fill some void in her life.

She's dressed in a pantsuit a size too big and it hangs heavily and loose around her body, disguising the womanly curves beneath.

"Do you want to sit?" she asks, gesturing with her pen that doesn't produce ink. Instead, it writes on a pad that uploads straight to her computer to file away for a later date. So sophisticated...

Why people feel the need to talk to a psychiatrist I will never understand. But it does serve my purpose. What harm can it do?

"I like your outfit," I lie, and I think she knows it. Her narrowed eyes trace the outline of my form.

"Yours is very pretty as well." Her genuine smile crinkles the lines around her eyes, showing her age.

Pretty.

A word on anyone else's lips but *his* is just a word.
Breathe.
My hands snake down the front of my dress and I almost feel pretty wearing it, but not quite.
Pretty little doll.
My fingers slide along the cool glass of the fish tank in the middle of the room. It's clear it's put there to make a statement, but all it tells me about this woman is she's lonely, *like me.* Only, I don't need to surround myself with pets that will die and be replaced to know this.

Out here in this big, bad world, I'm all alone.

She allows me to wander about her space and doesn't push me to sit or talk, so I take my time and eventually lower myself onto the seat opposite.

"How are you?" she asks.

What a simple, yet loaded question. *How am I?*

I'm scared. I'm angry. I'm lost.

"I'm missing a piece of me," I answer truthfully before flicking my gaze up to gauge her response.

Was she expecting such honesty? Would she see through the dress and hair to the broken doll beneath?

"Tell me about that. What are you missing?" She swirls her pen over the pad, but I can't see what it is she's writing. Her nose scrunches slightly and it makes me think she perceives more than I want her to.

She doesn't keep her eyes downcast and somehow manages to hold eye contact with me the entire time despite her subtle note taking.

"When I was a little girl," I say absently, my eyes drifting to the fish tank where a blue fish chases a yellow one, "my sister was fascinated with my hair. She used to braid plaits in either side and I used to let her. It helped to prevent tangles." I smile fondly, reminiscing in the memory.

"Tell me more about your sister, were you close?" The woman's interest is piqued and she leans slightly forward, as if she doesn't want to miss a single detail.

Her image flashes in my mind and I hold it there, terrified one day the memory of her face will fade and evade me forever. So perfect. Dark hair. Sparkling hazel eyes. Pretty.

Pretty little doll.

"Closer than anything," I whisper. My arms curl around my stomach. "Do you have some water?"

She points to a see-through jug holding water and what looks like sliced cucumber floating on top. "Help yourself."

I pour the water and a slice plops into the cup, causing some to jump out and wet the table.

"Sorry," I mutter, attempting to wipe it up with my hand. I don't belong in a stupid apartment that has fish as a feature drinking fancy water.

"It's fine, leave it." Leaning forward, she pats my hand and I jolt back into my seat. Her eyes widen and she holds up a hand in surrender. "I'm so sorry, you don't like to be touched?"

I do like to be touched…just not by strangers.

CHAPTER SEVEN

~ Flame Red ~

It's been three days since Bo left me and he's been ignoring my texts checking in on him, so that means I've been flying solo. It's hard to believe, but a sense of relief has settled over me. The fact that I am relieved that my boyfriend isn't curled up against me says a lot about my fucked up head. *And our fucked up relationship.*

Being alone without Bo's watchful eye has enabled me to go through the old case files. To pace around the living room when my anxiety wouldn't allow me to sleep.

I was free to think about Macy.

I may have peace where my home life is concerned, but I've been obsessing in a whole new fashion. I've been glued to my laptop searching. Always searching.

With my feet propped up on the coffee table, I scroll through yet another local doll making supply store. Benny was always so particular about the eyelashes and hair he purchased for the dolls. I learned this from when I ruined one of them and he bellowed, pacing my cell the next day, talking about how hard it would be to get the correct color to repair the patches I'd made.

Pretty hair for my pretty dolls.

Believe it or not, there are entire websites dedicated to doll hair alone. I've spent the better part of two days searching for ones within the vicinity of where they found me.

Earlier, while in the shower, I wondered about Benny. Would he truly leave his house and come for me? The thought of my sister all alone is too much to bear. I spent a good hour crying in the shower.

A sudden rap on my door jerks me to attention. I look down at my camisole and tiny shorts—not necessarily door answering material.

Maybe it's Bo.

Guilt sluices through me and carries me to my front door. I have a practiced apology on my lips when I fling it open. A dark shadow of a man stands on the shadowed entrance this man taller and broader than Bo. Without thinking, I bolt from the door toward my bedroom where I keep a Glock in my nightstand for emergencies. Chief took my department issued piece, but I'd be a fool not to protect myself.

As I run down my hallway, the front door slams and heavy footsteps thunder after me. I'm bent over, dragging my gun from the drawer, when a strong arm hooks my waist. I turn feral in his grip and claw at him the moment the gun slips from my hand. He forces me onto the bed, pinning both wrists to the sheets.

"Calm the fuck down, Jade."

Breathe.

I stop struggling and get lost in the chocolate eyes I hadn't seen in a few days.

Dillon.

"I thought you were..." I trail off, my voice hoarse.

"Him?"

Nodding, I take stock in the way he feels pressed against me, his powerful hips crushing my own. His grip on my wrists is painful and I know I'll be sporting bruises for days.

You're used to it. Benny would bruise you in the bed all the time, dirty little doll.

I squeeze my eyes shut and attempt to drive the madness out of my head. "I'm sorry I tried to kill you," I blurt.

Dillon chuckles, but doesn't release me. It causes his body to brush closer to mine and my nipples peak in reaction. When I reopen my eyes, he's staring at me with a look I've never seen from him before.

Want.

I think that's what the swirling in his eyes means, the heating of his cheeks and tongue darting out to dampen his bottom lip.

"Station's been lonely without you."

Still, he doesn't move.

Heat trickles just below my skin and I roll my eyes. "Nobody misses me there. They all hate the crazy girl."

He frowns as his eyes drop to my lips once again. It makes my heart thump loudly in my chest. "I missed you."

My mouth parts open in shock. Before I can reply, he lets me go and stands back up. I'm sprawled out on my back, my chest heaving and forbidden desire whirling through my veins. He skims his gaze over my breasts before giving a slight shake of his head, as if to clear it.

"Get dressed," he barks as he storms from the room. "I'm taking you to put some meat on that bony body of yours."

As soon as he leaves, I look down at my taut belly and hard nipples tenting the fabric. The camisole had ridden up, revealing my stomach flesh to him. A ripple of excitement courses through me.

Wait—did he say food?

I attempt to remember the last time I actually ate something and for the life of me, I can't recall. All those years in Benny's attic taught me how to survive on the bare minimum. Poor Bo thought it was his duty to keep me fed.

But Bo left you.

And now Dillon is going to feed you.

This time, I don't push away the shameful thoughts.

I enjoy each and every one of them as I dress.

I have an obsession with burgers. I squeeze the bun, spilling the oils and cheese out the side before stretching my mouth so wide, there's a slight sting in the corners, and devour each and every bite.

"Hungry?" Dillon muses, pushing his bowl of fries toward me. I help myself to one and dip it in my shake before shoveling it past my lips.

"It's not going anywhere," he says with a warm, deep laugh. "I can order you more."

"Benny fed us oatmeal and slop," I blurt, open and carefree.

Why was I letting my truth out? I didn't tell anyone this stuff. Not Bo. Not my parents. Not anyone.

"Is that all?" He tilts his head to the side, studying me.

Is that all? I have to hold in my disgusted laugh. We

weren't at fucking Disney camp.

"He was an appalling host," I mutter, stealing more of his fries.

"I've wanted to call you."

I pick up my shake and slurp on the straw, ignoring the stupid flip my heart just did.

"Really?" I smile behind the cup.

Pulling something from the bag he brought in the restaurant with him, he slides a document to me.

"The clothes on the doll."

My head swims as I pick up the piece of paper.

"They had your sister's DNA on them."

I drop it like it's on fire and stand abruptly, knocking the remainder of my shake to the floor. It seeps out, cold and unstoppable.

Just like Benny.

Macy.

The waitress hurries over, but Dillon puts his hand up to stop her approach.

"Blood?"

I'm dying inside. I left her. He killed her because of me.

"No," he assures and stands, taking my hand. "I promise. No blood. Everything is going to be okay, Jade. I swear it."

"It's not, though," I whisper.

Nothing is okay. Nothing will ever be okay.

"It was saliva and a hair."

I read the files of our case once I made it on the force. They had taken our hair and toothbrushes twelve years ago when the investigation got underway.

"It's a message," I choke, dropping back into the seat to stop myself from falling.

"He's been dormant as far as we know for the past eight years," he says. "What do you think could have caused the change?"

My head battles with my memories. All those years we were there and he killed until he thought I was ready for…

"She turned twenty-one a month ago," I murmur, the words feeling sticky in my mouth.

He stares at me, but I can't look him in the eye. "What does that mean? Why is that relevant?"

Crying, in the dead of night from Macy's cell, jerks me awake. Benny went to bed after leaving my cell and all has been quiet, so I know it's not because of him. Ever since he scarred Macy's face, he gets enraged when he looks at her, blames her for her new look and then punishes her with his belt. His fist. His hate.

"Jade," she whimpers. "Jade, I'm bleeding."

Rushing to the door, I place my hand there, dreaming of the day when our palms will touch again.

"Shhh, Macy," I urge, terrified she'll wake him.

He became angry with us talking one time and did the unthinkable. After binding us, he sewed our lips shut. I remember the way the needle burned as it tore through my flesh with such precision. After the first couple holes, I was numb to the pain—officially checked out mentally. The pain was crippling, but it was the scars that worried me most. He already treated Macy badly because of what he'd done to her face once before. I worried it would leave scars and he wouldn't want us anymore—that we'd finally be disposable to him. But Benny was an expert with a needle and thread and a few weeks later, the tiny holes healed over with the cream he put on them. Rubbing my finger over my lip, I shudder as I think of all the horrors we've faced while under his lock and key.

"I'm bleeding," *she sobs, and my entire body quivers with fear—fear he'll wake and punish his disobedient little dolls. In my peripheral, I see her hand push through her bars.*

"Where?"

"Between my legs," *she hisses.* "Am I dying, Jade?"

My heart breaks in two. Mom never had "the talk" with her about periods. She was too young at the time.

"It just means you're becoming a woman now," *I assure her, trying distractedly to keep the wobble out of my voice.* "It will be okay. I promise." *Another promise I can't keep.*

"A woman?"

"Yes. It happens to all girls eventually."

"Did it happen to you?" *She hiccups and sniffles.*

"Yes."

"So, I'm like you now?"

"Yes."

"Will Benjamin do those things to me now…the ones that make you happy?"

Happy? Shame marinates in my soul.

Will he?

"I'm not a pervert," *he barks, interrupting our exchange. Turning on his cot and getting to his feet, his cold eyes find mine.*

He stomps toward us and she whimpers with each step.

"You don't even have tits," he remarks, disgust in his clipped tone. "What have I told you about talking to each other?" Anger rolls just under his surface. I can almost see the steam coming off his skin. Like a demon straight from hell.

Looking in her cell, he tuts, "Look at that mess."

"Leave her alone, you asshole," I scream, rattling the bars like a trapped chimp.

His attention scans over to me and his feet carry him to my cell. "What?"

"Don't be a pervert, Benny," I growl, goading him. His eyes spark and he digs into his pocket, pulling out the key to my door. The door swings open and he takes a menacing step toward my retreating form.

"She's just a little girl." I shake my head in repulsion and his head jerks like I hit him.

"I wouldn't touch her like that," he snaps, his tone defensive. "I'm not a pervert."

Shaking my head, I snort. "You touched me like that."

"You're twenty-one," he barks in argument, smacking at his head with the palm of his hand.

"No, I'm not," I seethe. He squeezes his eyes shut and then springs them open, the pupils swallowing the dim color. "You look like you are," he growls, glaring at me. "I'm not a fucking pervert!" he bellows again. The monster of my world stomps toward me and swings his fist, connecting with my jaw. The impact takes me clean off my feet and I hit the cold floor with a thud.

Pain blazes through me, but I don't have time to register where before his boot collides with my ribs and a sick-

ening crack steals my breath. He drags me to my feet while I desperately gasp for air.

"No more," I wheeze.

I'm thrown to the bed, my body crumbling across it like a rag doll dropped from the hand of a spoiled child.

"I'm not a pervert," he hisses against the shell of my ear. The weight of his body suffocates me. My lungs roar for air and I gasp in broken puffs, getting nothing. His cock is inside me a moment later and his body thrusts against me, hard and feral.

"I'm not a pervert," he chants as he rapes me. I'm dying beneath him. Darkness fogs my eyes and my head spins. "Only you, little doll. I don't need another."

Gasp…gasp…nothing.

I wake on my bed, bandages wrapped around my abdomen and an ice pack on my face.

He didn't take me again, *until my face was pretty* again.

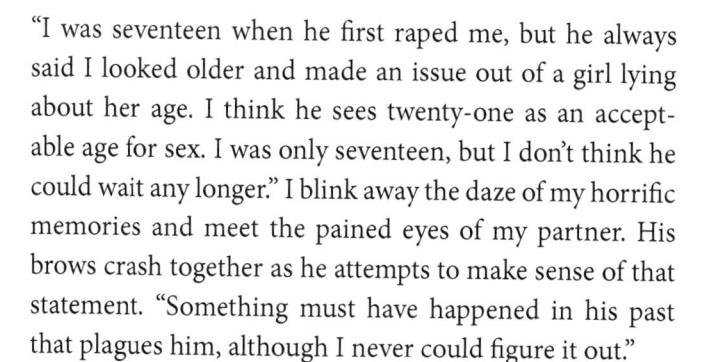

"I was seventeen when he first raped me, but he always said I looked older and made an issue out of a girl lying about her age. I think he sees twenty-one as an acceptable age for sex. I was only seventeen, but I don't think he could wait any longer." I blink away the daze of my horrific memories and meet the pained eyes of my partner. His brows crash together as he attempts to make sense of that statement. "Something must have happened in his past that plagues him, although I never could figure it out."

Dillon's jaw ticks and he draws his hands into fists as barely contained rage courses through him. "He's a fucking sick cunt. There's no excuse for what he did."

He's angry for me. Bo was always sad for me. I've never had a warrior in my court before. Not like this.

Dragging my eyes from his furious ones, I dig my fingernails into the skin of my forearms as I hug them to me.

Breathe.

"You think he will move on to her now?"

Her scar flashes in my mind.

"Ruined, ruined doll."

"Don't hurt her," I beg as I watch him get a dress ready for Macy.

"I'll make her pretty, but she'll never be perfect like you, dirty doll."

"No," I tell Dillon with conviction. "He would have waited for her to develop into a woman, but she still won't be enough for him because of her scar." My head shakes. "He'll seek a new doll for sexual gratification. That's what the other dolls were, the ones he killed. They were all older than us, and none were perfect enough." I let out a long sigh.

Why hadn't I put that together until now?

Because your head is fucked when it comes to him.

"So, we're looking at a possible future abduction." He glares at me. "And new murders if he doesn't find one he likes." He smashes a fist to the table, causing the dishes to rattle. "Fuck!"

"Or," I whisper, mostly to myself, "he's coming back for his dirty little doll."

"Dirty little doll?" Dillon flinches as he repeats the words.

"Me."

My bladder screams for relief. Giving in, I push the sheet away from my body and unwilling trudge to the bathroom. Raised voices alert me to more than just Dillon in my home. He brought me back here last night after I stormed out of the diner and insisted on getting drunk. We had no clues other than it being Macy's DNA and I couldn't deal with another night of pacing my place alone, so I drank until my legs felt weak and my heart didn't feel as hollow.

Dillon insisted on spending the night on the couch and I was too far gone to argue.

Still groggy, I swipe my hair from my face and pull my door open, making my way toward the noise. When I reach the scene, my eyes bug out of my head.

Bo is pinned against my kitchen wall by Dillon, who's in nothing but a fitted pair of black boxer shorts.

What the hell?

"How could you do this to us?" Bo shouts over the massive arm smashed against his chest.

Dillon lets out a growl.

"Nothing happened, Bo," I huff, waving away his aggression as nonsense. "This is my partner."

He laughs harshly, no humor present. "Jesus," he seethes, "you expect me to believe that when you're both practically fucking naked?"

My eyes lower to my unclothed form. Ever since my time with Benny, I've never been able to sleep with anything on. One pillow. A simple sheet. Bare. Just like I lived for four long years.

"It's not what it—"

"I fucked someone too," he blurts out, his tone scathing. He's trying to hurt me. Sadly, it doesn't like it should.

Relief.

"What?"

"Cindy, from my work. You know she's been after me since forever. Well, I fucked her after I left here the other night."

Cindy, ugh. She's the one who tried to steal a kiss from him at midnight at the New Year's Eve party last year. She's slutty and cheap.

Who is this man?

This isn't my devoted, doting Bo.

"You pushed me away," he says defensively. "You drove me to it. I came here to confess and hopefully move past it, but you have him here already. Did you fuck him in our bed?"

"My bed, Bo," I snap, but then soften my voice. I let tears form in my eyes as I speak words that will cut him. "And yes, I fucked him in my bed."

Dirty little doll.

"On my couch. In my shower. And that wall." I point to where he's still pinned by Dillon. Dillon grunts and flicks his eyes over his shoulder at me in confusion.

I will miss Bo. Learning to cope alone will be a task, but we just aren't supposed to be together. I'm toxic for him—stealing his hard earned happily ever after and drowning it in my dark past. Shit, Bo of all people cheated on me for God's sake. Loyal Bo, cheated on me. I drove him to it. I'm a mess.

"I want the ring back," he snarls, pushing at Dillon's

arm.

Dillon lets him go, but his body is still coiled and tense, eager to exact damage on Bo if he so much as looks at me wrong. When Bo starts toward me, Dillon shoves him out of the kitchen toward the front door. "Take it up with her over the phone. You're done here today, buddy."

"I want the goddamned ring back!"

I hold my hand up to calm him. Sadness picks away at my heart inside my chest. "You can have it. I'll send it to your mother's."

Our eyes meet once more and his lip curls in disgust—disgust at what he thinks I did to him. I want him to think I cheated. It will help his heart move on from me. He deserves more than I could ever give him, but my heart still aches because I'm losing my closest friend. He helped get me where I am today.

The door closes with a slam and I'm left staring at a half-naked Dillon. His eyes unabashedly skim over my bare form, his cock, long and generous, thickening in his boxers as he takes me in.

I should cover myself, but I don't.

Heat flushes my cheeks and causes my nipples to harden in response.

"We didn't fuck," he mutters, low and hoarse.

"I know," I breathe, my chest betraying my lust with heavy pants.

Dillon's gaze narrows, finally landing back on my face. "Put some fucking clothes on. We need to talk and I can't do that with you standing there looking so goddamned tempting."

Tempting?

I stare at him, dumfounded.

"Move your skinny little ass, Phillips," Dillon barks, "or I'm going to be talking to you with my cock nine inches deep inside your hot little body."

Nine?

I move my skinny little ass.

CHAPTER EIGHT

~ *Lava* ~

"Talk."

I peek over at him as he stirs one spoonful too many for my liking of sugar into his coffee. When I don't answer, he leans his hip against the kitchen counter and arches an eyebrow so I'll unload on him.

Thank God he's dressed.

And me too, for that matter.

My mind is still a jumbled mess at seeing my partner looking so…naked—so…alluring.

"Talk about what? About how I'm going to start pricking your finger to check your insulin levels while out in the field?" I say with a laugh, hoping to lighten the mood.

He sets his coffee down on the counter and takes a step forward until he crowds me with his heat. I tear my gaze from his intense one, but it's even worse staring at his solid chest through his white T-shirt while knowing how he looks underneath it. When I lift my eyes again, he smirks.

"Well, we should at least talk about this."

I laugh and go to push him away. His pecks are so firm. "There is no this." The man is like a brick pillar and doesn't move. Instead, he cages me against the wall—the very wall I told Bo he fucked me against. With both palms pressed beside my head, he leans in, brushing his mouth against my ear.

"Not what you told your boyfriend."

Swallowing, I attempt to push him from me, but again, he's immovable. "I needed to cut him loose." I feel like a bitch for saying the words. "It was a lie."

Dillon brushes his lips against my earlobe and a delightful shiver ripples through me. "Doesn't feel like a lie. Feels like a *this*, an us."

A mewl escapes me, to which he chuckles. *Asshole.* "He deserves better," I admit with a huff.

At this, Dillon becomes angry and pulls away to look at me. His face is furled into a scowl as he takes heavy breaths. "No, you deserve better. The motherfucker cheated on you at the first sign of trouble."

Tears prick my eyes. "I drove him to it. Because of how I am." My eyes fall to the floor in shame. I'll never be one-hundred percent right in the head for any man. I will never be able to fully devote myself to anyone as long as my sister remains that sick fuck's prisoner…and even then, am I too broken?

Strong fingers bite into my chin and my head is lifted. Dark, searing brown eyes pin me. "I've worked by your side for eight months, Jade. Eight goddamned months. You know what I saw?"

"A one-track minded bitch?" I laugh again, but my chest aches.

His eyes fall to my mouth briefly before lifting again. "I saw a good cop. Someone who, despite my ego, I fucking admired the hell out of. Someone who I wanted to protect because even though she was a hard ass, her eyes told otherwise. Not once did you look at any other man, even though they looked the hell out of you. You were faithful to that asshole and worked hard. He's the one who let something perfect fall through his fingers."

I gape at him, shocked by his words. "I, uh…" I stammer, "I'm not perfect."

"Who the hell is? Sure as hell not me. Definitely not ex-boyfriend, Bo. Perfect is in the eye of the beholder, Jade. In the right person's eyes, you're *all kinds* of perfect."

And that's *all kinds* of beautiful.

Jesus, when did Dillon become so sweet? So hot? So swoonworthy?

"Why are you being nice to me?" I ask, embarrassed tears threatening to fall.

One slips out and he cradles my face with his large hand. With a swipe of his thumb, he dries the tear. "Because you deserve it. Because maybe *I* see the perfect," he murmurs, his head dipping toward mine. "And for the first time in eight months, you let me in. I see you, Jade."

But can you handle what you see, Dillon?

"I don't like letting people in," I admit in a whisper. "They don't usually like what they see."

His nose brushes against mine and my eyes flutter closed. "You let me in. I really like what I see, and I don't plan on leaving any time soon."

Warm, soft lips press against mine. So gentle. Such a stark contrast from the hard, brooding partner I've dealt with from nine to five each day. When a strong hand grips my hip, I let out a sigh. His mouth coaxes mine open and his tongue seeks mine out. He tastes sweet, like the sugar he so heavily consumes.

His kiss is dizzying, but I don't want it to end. After the fallout with Bo, it's nice to still feel wanted—despite my raging flaws. Tentatively, I run my palms up his hardened chest to his shoulders. He takes it as an invitation to kiss me deeper, a low groan escaping him. With each delve of his tongue into my mouth, I grow lightheaded. The prickles of his five o'clock shadow scratch at my flesh in a way Bo's baby face never did. It feels different, and I like it—a lot. His kiss intoxicates me more so than Jack Daniels ever has.

He finally pulls away, eliciting a whine from me. A deep chuckle rumbles from his chest and he presses his forehead to mine, dark eyes locking in on me.

"What is this?" I ask heavily.

"This is real. This is how it should feel, Jade. This is perfect." And with that, he backs away and orders, "Put on some shoes. I'm taking you somewhere. I want to show you something."

I'm still heady and weak from our kiss. "Does this trip involve pancakes?" I question with a grin.

He winks at me. "I promised I'd fatten your skinny ass up. Now move, Phillips, before I carry you back there. And if I carry you to your bedroom," he says with a wolfish grin, "we're most definitely going to miss breakfast."

He turns into the gravelly drive of a dilapidated cemetery and the giant breakfast we consumed roils in my belly. When I risk a glance at him, his knuckles are white on the steering wheel and his jaw clenches. He drives toward the back of the small burial ground and shuts off the car once he's parked underneath a large oak. Thunder grumbles somewhere miles off, which means our little cemetery visit will be short lived.

"Why are we here?"

He gives me a grim smile and climbs out of the vehicle. His muscled back tightens as he takes long strides toward a headstone near the tree. It's the newest looking piece of granite in the entire fenced in area and fresh flowers poke out of the vase on top. I follow him over to it and read the name.

Delaney Scott
November 14th, 1981 - May 3rd, 2010
Beloved daughter and sister

Frowning, I place my hand on his hard shoulder. "Is that—"

"My little sister," he confirms. "She would have turned thirty-five this year."

I slide my hand down until I grip his with mine. After our kiss and the playful flirting at breakfast, it feels right to comfort him this way.

"I'm sorry."

He turns to look at me, pain flashing in his molten chocolate orbs. "Me too."

"What happened?"

Anger ripples through him. I start to pull my hand from his grip at the sudden change of his mood, but he tightens it and turns his hardened gaze to mine. "Some asshole she dated. Chip was his name. I fucking hated that guy. Always knew my sister was better than his sorry ass."

I frown at his words. "Did he hurt her?"

He scoffs. "Hurt? He did more than hurt her. Jade, he fucking destroyed her. The guy was a lowlife. Drugs, alcohol, petty crime. He was a loser and she was consumed by him. He made her promises and she believed every one of them. It wasn't long before we didn't even recognize her anymore. He got her hooked on heroin and knocked her up."

A gasp leaves me as the first drop of rain splashes on to my cheek.

"She managed to get clean and I warned that fucker to stay away and he did, or so I thought." He shakes his head, looking to the ground. "I had no fucking idea he liked to beat up on women."

Shuddering, I think of all the times Benny struck me. A thunderclap in the distance makes me jump in surprise.

Dillon runs his free hand through his dark hair and lets out a hiss of air as if it pains him to tell me this. "On Jasmine's first birthday…"

I raise a brow. *Jasmine?*

"My niece."

A genuine smile reaches all the way to his eyes, but it's fleeting.

"He showed up and fed Laney a load of bullshit about being clean and changing his ways."

Gritting his teeth, he looks at me. "Lies. The bastard—he hit her a little too hard. And when he realized he'd gone too far and fucking murdered my sister, he fled. The motherfucker didn't even try to get her help or notify the authorities. He left Jasmine in her room and just disappeared."

Hate radiates from him and he breaks from my grip to kneel down at her head stone. His powerful hand grips the granite as he bows his head. I allow him his moment of silence as a storm of thoughts brew in my head just as quickly as the one closing in on us.

Did they find Chip?

Is he in jail for murder?

Where's Jasmine?

Lightning followed by a loud thunderclap jerks Dillon out of his moment and he stands. Fat rain drops begin to pelt down on us and his white T-shirt quickly becomes soaked, revealing his sculpted torso beneath. We don't run to the car. Instead, we stand in the pouring rain, staring at one another. With two quick strides, he eats up the distance between us, spears his fingers through my hair, and tilts my head up to look into his angry eyes.

"I searched for him tirelessly for almost three years. Three long years I spent every evening and weekend hour doing what my own department failed to do." He leans his forehead against mine. "I obsessed over this shit. I wanted justice for Delaney and to know he could never come for Jasmine."

My chest aches for him, but I know exactly how he feels. "Did you find him?"

A low growl escapes him. "I found him. Found him in some shit motel in another state. Tracked his ass all the way to Nebraska."

"Did you get your justice?" Our eyes meet and understanding flashes through us like electricity from the storm soaking us to the bone.

"He died from a heroin overdose. His body was

found with a rubber band tied around his arm and a needle hanging from his vein. Nobody called for help. Nobody fucking cared. Two days before they found him." My fingers flutter over his soaked chest heaving with fury.

"You made him pay. He deserved it." My words are but a whisper, getting lost in the howling winds.

His lips hover over mine, the only warmth in the chilly rain shower. "Finding Chip was my only thought. My only care. My motherfucking reason for living. And now that he's gone, a weight has been lifted. He got what he deserved. Watching his eyes widen with fright as I shoved the needle into his arm was the highlight of my whole damn life. Then watching him drain from this world into the depths of hell became my new favorite moment."

Yanking at his T-shirt, I pull him to me and our lips crash together with fury. His large hands find my ass and grip me so hard, I know I'll be bruised for days. A needy moan pours from my mouth into his as he devours me.

A deafening crack of thunder jolts us away from each other and he steals my hand as we run back to the car. Once inside, safe from the storm, he narrows his gaze at me.

"I know how it feels, Jade. What you see as a social disability is something I can understand with each part of my poor broken heart. I'm not some pussy who gets his panties in a wad when his girl fights for justice."

My heart flutters at his words. "Who are you then?"

A smile blooms on his soft lips. "I'm your partner," he says, and then his voice lowers. "And I'm your friend. Hell, I may even be more than that if you keep kissing me like that, woman. But one thing is for certain…"

I blink at him, my eyes darting between his in question. "What's that?"

"I'm going to help you get your justice. We're going to find your sister and that fuckface who took you two."

"And then?"

A murderous scowl passes over his features. "And then, we're going to do much worse than shove a needle in his vein. We're going to make him pay for every goddamned thing he ever did to you."

Hope, for the first time in forever, blossoms inside me. Could we really track that psycho down like he tracked down his sister's killer? Will this all finally be over soon?

"Together, Jade," Dillon says, his voice grumbling like the thunder above us. "We do this together, every step of the way."

"Think these two are linked?" I question, shoving two newspaper articles across my kitchen table toward him.

Dillon picks them both up and scans them. "Two young teens. Missing, but not thought to have run away. Bodies later found strangulated. Hmmm," he says, his eyes narrowed, "doesn't seem like his MO."

I know I'm reaching. For eight years, all I've done is reach. Hence the reason I have five gigantic boxes full of articles about missing girls all over the US, including the ones my parents collected the four years I was missing. "You're right. Benny doesn't strangle them. He mutilates them."

My stomach grumbles and Dillon chuckles, breaking the tension some. "I'm ordering pizza for dinner. Those damned pancakes are long gone from this big boy's belly. You're a slave driver, Phillips. I don't even work through lunch at the precinct."

A smile graces my lips and I glance over at him. After the cemetery visit, we swung by his modest home on the outskirts of town so he could shower and change clothes. It was his day off and he was spending it bringing me up to date on the case so far. We'd driven past a flea market and it was lively with people. But experience told me that even though we were taken on a Saturday from a hellhole like that one, it was a fruitless endeavor to go. Most of the vendors were regulars and after years of interrogating everyone there, I'd pretty much been banned from coming back. Dillon had slowed, but I waved him on. There were no answers there on a Saturday.

He steals my laptop to place the order. After a few moments, his brows furl together. "Check this out. When I pulled up local events between here and your hometown, several crafting fairs pulled up. Some even advertise doll vendors. Have you checked into any of these?"

Climbing out of my seat, I rush over to him and lean in, placing my hands on his shoulders so I can view the screen better. His clean body wash scent envelops me and I inhale it. The smell is comforting and I instantly take a liking to it.

"Are any of the vendors called Benny's Pretty Dolls?" I shudder just saying the name of his booth. "Benjamin is another name it could be under."

He scrolls down the list of the vendor names. When he makes it to the J's, we both point at the same time. Doll with the Jade Eyes.

A shiver ripples through me. "Do you think?"

Turning, he looks over his shoulder at me and I see the hope dancing in his eyes too. "Very well could be. I mean, you don't have green eyes, but your name is Jade. Too close to ignore."

I smile broadly at him, fat tears welling in my eyes. "Oh my God. What if it's him? What if we finally find Macy?"

He stands up and pulls me to him for a hug. Bo always wanted me to run from my past, yet here's Dillon—so strong and passionate—running with me toward it.

"We're gonna find her, Jade. The craft fair opens at ten on Monday and is in town until Friday. I'll take my lunch break at eleven. Meet me at the station and we'll ride over there together. The two of us can take his ass down if it comes to it."

Nodding, I agree and press a chaste kiss to his handsome mouth. "Thank you."

I start to pull away, but his fingers thread into my hair and he deepens our kiss. He's hard between us and desire licks at my flesh with the need to explore him. Thankfully, he's the stronger willed of the two of us and tears from our heated kiss. A need that matches my own flickers in his eyes.

Benny always took what he wanted.

Bo was always so gentle and asked what I needed.

And Dillon steals kisses. His touch is rough and bruising, yet he doesn't ever do anything I'm not equally hungry for.

For once, I find myself desiring a man like never before. The playing field is equal—two partners navigating a messy path together.

"I'm going to run out and pick up some beer while the pizza is on its way," he says gruffly, stepping away from me.

My eyes fall to his jeans where his hardened cock makes the fabric bulge. "Are you staying the night again?"

He growls and it makes me shiver in delight. "I'll stay one more night. On the sofa. Alone."

Our eyes meet and his need for me is unmasked. It rages like the fiery sun.

"You don't want…" I can't bring myself to finish. A small pout forms on my lips.

His chuckle is sexy and it drives me crazy. "Woman, I want you. Believe me. But know this about me," he says as he scoops his keys from the table by the front door, "once I start, I don't stop. The moment I have you underneath me, I'm going to want to spend every waking second tasting your milky flesh. And right now, we have shit to focus on besides each other." He winks at me before the door slams shut behind him.

Cold realization showers over me and I fall into his chair at the table. We're going to investigate our only lead the day after tomorrow, which means we need to do more research. Tomorrow, I'll need to study the different exits of the craft fair and other vendors. We certainly don't need to be laid up in bed, no matter how good that sounds right now.

Macy is still out there.

Sex with this god of a man can most definitely wait.

It has to.

There's only one man I can focus on right now.

Benny.

Bloated and blurry eyed, my head lulls to the side and I jerk, catching myself. The chuckle from Dillon draws my eyes. He's on his second beer and I've lost count of his number of slices of pizza. One beer and two slices has me ready for bed, but I refuse to give in.

"You should get an early night," he suggests, but I shake my head and wave my finger back over the icon on my laptop.

"I'm good."

I search Google Maps for the hundredth time around the area I was found. It's just trees for miles and then some private land with nothing on it.

"I'll be visiting my mom and Jasmine tomorrow," Dillon announces.

My eyes lift from the screen to eye his over the top.

"It's why I don't work weekends," he explains, a sheepish smile on his handsome face. Guilt infects me for always bitching at him about being a typical nine to fiver.

He places his bottle down on the table and grabs a new one, holding it up to me. I shake my head no and he leans back, holding me in his intense gaze. "I'm all they have. My dad passed away a year ago and my mom took it hard." His brow furrows and he looks intently at the bottle in his hand, mindlessly peeling the sticker from it. "I like to do things with Jasmine—make up for her not having parents to do that stuff with her. My mom's amazing, but she's getting older now and needs the break."

I still can't believe I used to think he was an asshole

for not working weekends. I'm officially a major bitch. He's wonderful and I'm the asshole for not seeing it sooner. I've had my blinders on for far too long.

"That's a great thing, Dillon," I tell him with a smile. "She's lucky to have you." It's all I can do to stop myself from throwing my laptop down and darting across the room so I can straddle him like he's a mechanical bull and I need to hold on for dear life.

"If you don't want to be alone, you could come."

His body coils tight and the veins in his arms bulge, making my mouth water. The tick in his jaw shows how tense he is, but I'm unclear whether it's because he wants me to go or he's only asking out of pity.

"I actually visit my parents on Sundays," I tell him, and he doesn't question the lie.

The last place I want to go is back there, especially with Bo holed up next door with his folks.

Nodding his head once firmly, he tips the bottle to his lips and picks up the file he was looking over. I lower my eyes back to the laptop screen, hating the silence that's descended upon us. My eyes grow heavy as the screen burns my retinas, and then I'm drifting.

Something is wrong. Benny keeps looking at us in our cells while pacing. Nerves eat away at my insides with every urgent peek he takes.

"Did you drink your water?" he barks at me.

"Yes," I lie, and he studies me with those hollow eyes.

"You're lying to me," he snarls, his eyes narrowing.

"Why do you care whether I've drank anything?" I

smart mouth, and then swallow as the fight in me ebbs with every ragged breath he takes.

"You little cunt."

A gasp explodes from my chest as my feet retreat to the corner of the room.

Clank.

No...

"You think you can defy me?" he roars, stepping inside my hell with me. "Where is the bottle?"

Why the hell is he so furious? I just wanted to save the water. My eyes flick to the pillow he allowed me to have and then back to him. A flash in his eyes and the curling of his lips tells me he saw my not so subtle look.

He marches over and throws my pillow from the bed, grabbing the bottle. "Come here."

"No."

He spins so fast, it makes me dizzy. Marching over to where I'm huddled in the corner, he grabs me around the throat. On instinct, my hands claw at his wrist as I try in vain to loosen his hold.

"Dirty little defiant doll," he growls, scraping my back across the wall, causing a sharp burn to ignite the skin.

"Fuck you," I snarl, pulling all the saliva from my mouth and spitting it at him. There's nothing he can do to me that he hasn't already done apart from killing me. And at this point, I think I'd welcome it.

A flare of pain explodes in my ankle as his foot collides with mine with such force, my legs part. If it weren't for him holding me up, I'd have dropped into the splits.

Before I can truly register the pain, he sneers at me. "No, fuck you."

He wiggles the water bottle before making a vulgar show of sucking on the screwed on cap. Then, with a brutal shove, he begins penetrating my body with it. It's too big for my small opening and doesn't go in far, but it doesn't stop him from trying. Over and over again. A relentless stabbing attempt to shove the plastic into my body.

Pain burns and rips at every nerve ending there, but I'm powerless to end it and my screams are muted by the tightening of his hand around my throat.

"You got something to say now?" he mocks, finally jerking it out of me.

Warm liquid runs down my leg and he brings the bloody bottle to his mouth. I want to die. Just kill me already!

He unscrews the lid with his teeth and shoves the bottle against my lips, pouring the contents into my mouth.

Copper-tinged water cascades over my lips and tongue, but his hold prevents it from going down my gullet. I choke and gurgle and spit the water everywhere.

Ding-dong.

My eyes flare wide and his mimic mine.

Someone's here? That was a doorbell?

My mouth opens wide as adrenaline pumps through me. Bringing my head toward his, he bares his teeth at me before he fires it back and my skull connects with the wall, stealing my consciousness.

Everything is black.

My eyes open and everything is black. There's nothing but darkness all around and a heavy weight rests on top of me.

No! No! No!

"No...*no!*" I battle the suffocation, kicking and writhing, and then a flash of light burns my eyes as Dillon's voice penetrates the fear.

"It's okay," he says in a soothing tone. "You're safe."

Pushing the heavy weight to the floor, I jump to my feet, panting and looking down at the enemy.

It's a quilt. It's just a freaking quilt.

"You fell asleep. I moved you to your bed and found something to cover you up with," he says, his voice calm, holding his hands up in surrender.

Damn, I'm a mess. He must think I'm crazy.

My heart rate slows and I swipe the sweat from my forehead. "I'm sorry," I choke out, a sob lodged in my throat.

All the insecurities, all the abuse, all the tough cop act I put on everyday floods from me like a virus sweating itself from the body.

All the pent up fear and agony seeps out and I gasp for air, for something to ground me. Dillon's hot palm engulfs mine and I'm pulled into his body as his arms snake around me, pinning me to him. His scent envelops me and I suck to inhale it, to cover myself in him, inside and out—to erase Benny and the dream.

You dreamed of him.

Something passes between us in this moment. It's not a partner comforting a partner. It's not a friend soothing a friend. It's another human sharing your pain, understanding the silent moments as well as the loud ones. It's two souls touching the essence of each other. It's a man holding a woman and showing her it's okay to break because he will keep her together until she can do it for herself.

I come undone in this moment, and he lets me, taking all my anger, fear, and pain into himself.

"We'll catch him and end this for you. I promise," he repeats with more conviction than I've ever heard before, from anyone.

Lifting me on to the bed, he cradles me and we fall asleep cocooned together. For the first time in my life, I feel truly safe.

CHAPTER NINE

~ Rust ~

"I'M GLAD YOU CAME AGAIN." This woman with her fish tank office decoration and pantsuit scrutinizes me with narrowed blue eyes. "Please, have a seat when you're ready."

I run my fingers over the back of the brown sofa and the soft leather feels cool on my fingertips. "How old are you?"

She frowns and it makes her look much older. "Is age important to you? How old are you?"

Ignoring her question, I make my way over to the strange cucumber water. It reminds me of something a girl and her dollies would have at a tea party like the ones we used to have with our mother. I pour the chilly liquid into a glass and take a small sip.

"Do you have any friends?" she questions.

I sneak a peek at her. Her finger grips the pen she uses for her device and her bushy eyebrow lifts nearly to her hairline.

A sad sigh escapes me. "Not many," I admit. "But I don't want any."

She sits up and gazes at me, compassion flickering in her bright blues. "Why don't you want any, doesn't everyone?"

My laughter echoes in the quiet room. "No."

I watch her features to see if my words affect her. They do. Disappointment wrinkles her brow for a brief moment before she masks it with indifference.

"Let's talk about you. Last time you were here, you mentioned a sister. Do you have any other siblings?"

I cringe at the mention of my sister. Not one day goes by where I don't think about her. That I don't close my eyes and try to remember the sound of her comforting voice.

"No."

She lets out an exasperated sigh. It's soft, but I hear it. I always notice the tiniest of details. It's what makes me so good at what I do.

"I can't help you if you don't talk to me," she says finally, and her eyes skim to the clock on the wall.

I sit down on the sofa and take my time looking her over. Age and her profession, where she sits all day, has seemed to add wrinkles and at least twenty pounds to her already curvy figure. The picture she has on her website reveals a vibrant, younger, and much thinner woman. Seems I'm not the only one who wishes she were someone else.

"I don't need help," I tell her with a slight bite to my voice. What could she do for anyone?

She frowns. "You wouldn't be here if you didn't."

Shrugging, I gulp down the cold beverage. When I'm finished, I set my glass down on the decorative book on the table that wasn't here last time. Moving my eyes to meet hers, she flinches, but doesn't say anything. Satisfied, I lean back against the cushions.

"I come here because he asked me to."

"Who is he? Your boyfriend?"

My boyfriend…*no*, but what exactly are we?

"You hold affection for this man," she establishes.

"Yes, always," I tell her honestly.

She smiles, and it's genuine. It makes her seem younger. Prettier.

Pretty little doll.

CHAPTER TEN

~ Rosewood ~

It was a Saturday when I was taken, but it felt just like this. The same stifling heat. Same bustling bodies reeking of musky body odor.

Why did you come back here?

I thought I should stay true to what I told Dillon about visiting my parents, but instead, my car turned off at the dirt road I used to walk down every Saturday afternoon.

The sun licks at my bare arms and burns against the black pants I put on. I'm standing, looking down at the book booth I used to visit each time. The same woman from all those years ago still runs it. It's like the place was frozen in time.

Macy and I were never allowed to come on Sundays like today. Sundays were for church. Many times I wished church was on Saturday too. Maybe then we would have never have met Benny.

"You a reader?" the woman enquires, nodding down to a set of worn Harry Potter books.

Shaking my head, I get right to the point. "Are there any doll booths here? There used to be one here."

She stills, not looking up from a stack of books before

she begins laying them out on the table.

"Are you a reporter? Because that story has been done to death," she gripes with an annoyed shake of her head.

That story. Like it's one of her fiction novels.

That story I endured for four years.

That story was as real as it was horrific.

"Actually," I lie through gritted teeth, "I'm just looking for a gift for someone."

Her head lifts and she points through the crowd of people. "There's a toy booth a hundred yards that way. You'll find something there, I'm sure."

"Thanks."

She doesn't acknowledge my appreciation. Instead, she turns to talk to another customer as they approach.

My feet carry me to said booth and my heart pounds.

I should feel close to Macy here, but I don't. All I feel is how much I failed her.

"Hey there, sugar," a deep, raspy voice drawls. He sounds like he's smoked a pack a day his entire life.

My eyes lift up to see a giant of a man. He's covered in tattoos, his thick greying beard hangs nearly halfway down his pudgy gut, and he's tilting his head to check out my ass.

"Whatcha looking for?"

Running my fingers against the cloth he has over one of the tables littered with toys, I ignore him. He eventually tuts and stalks over to a little girl with her mother.

"Pretty doll for a pretty doll," I hear him say and almost drop the teddy bear I've picked up.

Scanning the child, I notice a porcelain doll huddled against her chest.

"Can I have it, Mommy, please?"

My feet carry me over to them and before I can stop myself, I'm pulling the doll from her arms. The girl gasps in shock.

"Excuse me," her mother snaps.

"Where did this come from?" I demand, waving the doll to the toy vender.

He scratches a hand over his bald head and stares at the doll, shrugging his shoulders. "It's not one of mine. She must have picked it up somewhere else." He eyes the girl's mom. "Where did she find this?"

"Right there." Her mother points to the table in front of us.

"Does it have a sticker on it?" he asks, reaching for the doll. I step away from him and check the foot where Benny used to put the prices.

Twenty-eight dollars.

Thud.

Thud.

Thud.

"That's not right," he grumbles. "It's worth twice that."

Benny.

"It must be from the stock my wife put out," he lies, clearly just wanting to make a profit.

A flare of auburn hair and hazel eyes catch my eye through the crowd and all the noise mutes to nothing. My heartbeat thunders in my ears.

Macy?

A firm grip encloses around my bicep. The man has come around the table and is holding me, lifting my arm. "The doll," he demands. My hand unclasps the doll and he drops my arm to grab it. A smash ricochets behind me as I dart through the crowd of people in search of those hazel eyes.

"You're paying for that," he hollers from behind me. "Hey! Come back here!"

My body collides roughly with other people as I push through them.

Macy.

The dirt beneath my feet kicks up as I scramble to get to her. My eyes burn as I try to keep them from blinking.

Macy.

A smile I recognize flashes through the thin veil of her hair. So brief. Just one glimpse.

"Move!"

"Excuse me!"

"Sorry, I need to get through!" I grasp out toward her. She's within reach and her hair sways as her body moves.

"Macy!" I shout, spinning her by the shoulder to face me.

Disappointment floods into my soul. A wide-eyed girl stares back at me, confused.

She's not Macy.

Opening my mouth but having no words to speak, my body jars when a hand jerks me around.

"Hey." I don't have an immediate reaction to being manhandled, I'm too gutted that she wasn't Macy.

"You need to pay for breaking that doll." The man from the toy stall growls.

It wasn't even his doll. *Asshole.*

With a huff, I shove my hand into my jeans, pull out a couple twenties, and chuck them at his chest. When he snatches for them, I grab his thumb and bend it back until it pops.

"Shit!" he bellows. "You crazy bitch!"

"Don't ever touch me again," I hiss through gritted teeth before leaving him there with his dislocated thumb.

Sitting in my car, I watch every single person who leaves the market, but I don't see *her*. It was my mind playing games with me. Again.

That poor woman I grabbed must have thought I was crazy.

You're certifiable.

Was that doll a coincidence or is he playing mind games with me?

He wouldn't know you'd come here.

When the vendors pack up and the place is empty, I start up the car and drive to the spot where I was hit by the truck the day I ran away from Benny.

The woman, Ellie Russell, who hit me passed away a couple years ago. Cancer ate away at her colon. She had visited my bedside every day while I was recovering. Later, I learned she was on her way to pick up her granddaughter when she hit me. "I've never been so pleased to run someone down," she always joked to me and anyone else who would listen.

As I drive to that location, I take note of my surroundings. The trees are so tall and green. There's a tremor in my hand just looking into the abyss. These woods went on forever. I could have easily become lost in them and died from the elements alone. Once I'm at the exact spot

I was hit, I pull over and stare off into the direction Ellie had said I came from.

Where are you, Macy?

Tap! Tap! Tap!

I startle when knuckles rap at my car window.

Checking the mirror, I see a truck has pulled up behind me. I was so zoned out on the woods, I wasn't paying attention to anything else.

I push the button to roll down the window. No sooner do I have it rolled down, a large hand wraps around my neck, squeezing, restricting.

"You crazy little bitch."

The man from earlier has his arm in my car and me by the throat.

Just like Benny used to.

My lungs burn and my stomach muscles tense, fighting along with me for air.

Stretching my hand, I power up the window, trapping his arm and forcing him to release me.

Hot, white anger explodes behind my eyes.

How dare he touch me.

No one will ever touch me like that again.

Opening the door with a hard shove, I push him back with his arm still caught. *Dick.* Serves him right. I clamber out of the car on a mission and he reaches for me with his free arm. The man's easily six-foot-four, but he doesn't have a gun.

Bending, I snatch my Glock from the holster strapped to my ankle and point it directly at him. His hostile posture quickly changes to surrendering victim.

"Don't shoot me," he begs. "I just wanted to teach you

a lesson." As if that will make what he did any less violent and a freaking crime.

"What lesson would that be?" I ask, my hand firm, the blood inside my veins sizzling and vibrating with the need to punish.

He shakes his head, tugging to free his jammed arm.

"*Well?!*" I scream.

Dragging his arm from the binds of the window and frame, he screeches and rubs down the now sore, scraped skin.

"I'm just going to get in my truck," he tells me with his arm cradled to his chest. His feet shuffle in a semi-circle three feet around me. I turn with him, keeping the gun pointed at his head.

We both hear the engine, but it's too late. As his head turns to see the oncoming truck, it hits him, taking him up in the air like he weighs nothing. Blood spatters my face, causing me to gasp in surprise. My hand shakes, still holding my weapon out in front of me.

Thump.

His body hits the asphalt like a bag of meat being thrown from a bridge. The truck doesn't stop. It just drives away and I can't move. I'm solidified to the spot I'm standing in. Then, my body does the unthinkable. It's moving into the driver's seat and I'm driving away, leaving him there dying…or dead.

I turn the lights on and watch them illuminate the road before me.

Red…blue…red…blue…red…

"Dispatch, Phillips two thirty-one."

"Go ahead, Phillips two thirty-one."

"I have a four-eighty. I'm in pursuit of the vehicle, traveling south on Route Nine, requesting eleven forty-one."

"Copy that, Phillips. Hit and run. You're in pursuit. You have a victim with severe injuries."

"Affirmative."

"Copy that. Ambulance en route."

Putting my foot down to gas my vehicle, I rub the blood spray from my face as best I can and try not to think about leaving the hit-and-run victim in the middle of the road.

He deserved it.

The truck is too far ahead and fading from view. Then it's gone. Like it grew wings and flew away. I slow down when I come to the point where I lost him and search the wooded area for a dirt road, but there are only trees—one broken and fallen over. Son of a bitch.

"Dispatch."

"Go ahead."

"I lost the vehicle," I grumble. "Returning to the victim."

"Copy that."

My car slows and my head spins. There's no one here. No truck. No guy.

Oh my God, am I losing my mind?

Sirens blast in the distance, getting closer and closer to my insanity.

My head is fuzzy as I seek answers in the asphalt, my heart pumping twice as fast as it should be.

"Phillips, what do we have?" Jefferson questions as he and Michaels trot over to stand beside me with their hands on their pistols still holstered on their hips. I didn't call for back up, but it's not unusual for other officers to respond. The ambulance arrives a few seconds later and I'm still standing there, dumbfounded. "Phillips?"

"I'm not crazy," I defend.

They glance at each other and then back to me.

"I swear, the truck hit him and he …" My feet stomp the asphalt as my arms gesture to where he hit the ground. "Look," I bark. *There's blood. I'm not crazy.*

"Maybe he got up and took off."

"No…no. He was…" *Dead.* A hand comes down on my shoulder and I jump, spinning around and swinging my fist out in front of me.

"Calm your shit, Phillips. It's adrenaline. I've seen a man hit a pillar, get out of the car with a bone hanging out his leg, and sprint up the road. Shock does crazy things to a person."

They're walking back to their vehicle.

"We can put out an APB," Jefferson says. "You get a good look at the vic or suspect?"

"Victim is a white male and bleeding to death," I deadpan.

I climb back in my car and pull away. They're both waving their hands in the air and mouthing, "What the fuck?"

They must have passed him if he did get up and drive away. He won't get far. There's no way he's not badly damaged from that hit. Hell, I'm wearing half his blood.

"No, Detective. Nobody of that description."

I disconnect from the fifth hospital I've called. No one has come in or been taken in with the asshole's description. Maybe he was okay. Maybe he has a high pain tolerance.

He screeched at a little arm scrape.

There's no way. He's dead. I just have to find the body.

Grabbing a bite of cold pizza left over from last night, I chew and swallow before gulping down a bottle of water.

Bang! Bang! Bang!

I set the water down with a whispered, "Fuck," and draw my gun from its holster.

"It's Dillon, Jade. Don't fucking shoot me."

I bite my lip to stop the laugh that wants to erupt from my chest. He knows me so well. Placing my gun on the console table, I unchain the door and swing it open. It hasn't even been a whole night since I've seen him, but it feels like a lifetime. My instincts are to throw myself into his arms, but I stop myself, not clear what the dynamics of this thing between us are.

I don't have to wait long, though. His worried eyes scan my face and then his heavy boots eat up the space between us, pulling me in to his heady embrace.

I swim in his decadent scent and melt into him like ice on a fire. "I missed you," I murmur, the words slipping from my tongue before I can stop myself.

"I was out all day. I didn't have my cell so I didn't know." He pulls back and grasps my face in his palms, the pads of his thumbs stroking down the apples of my cheeks. "What happened? You witnessed an accident? What were you doing out there?"

"Some prick followed me from the flea market."

I grab his hands, but they don't move.

"Who is he?"

"No one. Just some asshole." I shrug and tilt my lips up into a defeated smile. I'm exhausted.

"Did he do anything to you?" He penetrates my eyes with his own, seeking and delving beyond the surface. "Jade?" His voice is pained as his hands fall from my face.

I flick my hair over my shoulders and show him the bruising I discovered around my neck earlier.

"Motherfucker. Who was he? I don't understand," he says with a growl, his eyes traveling from my neck to my eyes and back again. "Did he hurt you anywhere else?"

"No," I assure him as I move to close the door. I clutch onto his hand and drag him through to the living space. "I was going to my parents' and found myself at the flea market." My gaze flickers over to his, expecting to see annoyance, just like I'd see with Bo each time I'd accidentally find myself there. Dillon doesn't seem angry, though. He sighs as he sits on my couch, dragging me down to sit on his lap. I curl into him, letting his breathing regulate my own.

"Go on," he urges.

"I broke a doll and the vendor got pissed at me. He put his hands on me, so I dislocated his thumb." I shrug and nuzzle into his neck. His chest moves with a jolt and I lift my head to peek at him. A perfect flash of his white teeth greets me. "Are you laughing at me?"

"I'm just happy you can look after yourself." Pride ripples through him and it makes its way into my heart. "Go on, Wonder Woman."

Rolling my eyes, I continue my story. "Well, then he

followed me. I was too distracted to notice him. He managed to grab me, but I pulled my gun on him. It was then that a truck came from nowhere and slammed into him. I heard the popping of his bones. His blood sprayed my face." A shudder ripples through me as I remember that last part. "And then he was just gone. Vanished."

"Maybe the shock from the accident had him driving off…" he trails off and I collapse back against him. *Maybe.*

"How was your day?" I question, changing the subject.

"It was great. Jasmine is a firecracker. Just you wait until you meet her, Jade. She's a take no prisoners kinda gal. A lot like you." He kisses my head and the joy in his tone is genuine and beautiful.

He wants me to meet his niece. Maybe he doesn't think I'm crazy. Better yet, maybe he doesn't care that I am.

CHAPTER ELEVEN

~ Scarlet ~

*B*LURB, BLURB, BLURB.

Is that all they do in there? Are they supposed to be therapeutic? Because they're not. I want to flick one to see if that's just air in its bloated tummy.

"You like the fish?" She's not in a pantsuit today. Today, she's wearing a shin-length skirt. Looks like she's retaining water in her ankles, and she knows it if the shifting of her feet because I'm looking at them are any indication.

I don't answer her. It's pointless. She's clearly a fraud if she can't determine whether I like her stupid fish or not.

"Tell me more about this man," she urges. "You said he was bleeding in the road."

"The world is a crazy place. Sometimes I wonder if I ever even left my cell. Maybe this is all in my head. A weird, taunting dream," I ponder as she scurries to write on her device.

"This is the first time you've mentioned a cell. Can you tell me about what it was like for you in there?"

I run my finger along a pleat in my skirt. "Hot in the summer—like sweat dripping, mind fuzzing heat. And then in the winter months, it was freezing. The pipes used to creak whenever a tap was turned on somewhere in the house."

"So, it was a house you were kept in."

Is she trying to trick me? What else would it be?

"They used to sound like wolves howling at the moon. I sometimes used to make up stories that he was a werewolf." I laugh, lost in thought.

"He?"

Oh God, she really is terrible at her job.

"Times up," I announce.

And hopefully it will be soon.

CHAPTER TWELVE

~ Ruby ~

I CHECK THE CLOCK AGAIN, tapping at the dash to make sure it's working correctly and then look down at my cell phone.

11:37.

Damn him. When he left me this morning, he said he would meet me at this craft fair at eleven instead of me meeting him at the precinct, so where the hell is he?

"I've waited long enough," I mutter to myself before slipping from my car and making my way over to the bustling fair.

Booth after booth line the huge stretch of green. Finding the stall we looked up on Saturday night is going to be a task.

Stopping by the first booth selling all kinds of different cheeses, I hand them the printout of the booth name and banner they use, and he shakes his head no.

I repeat the process over and over until familiarity flashes in a fabric seller's eyes.

"He's set up four booths to the right. Jonny or something," the seller tells me, scratching at his head like an ape.

"Thanks," I tell him, snatching the flyer back.

"Benny!" he shouts, stopping me in my tracks and turning my insides to stone.

"What did you say?" My words are almost inaudible.

"Benny," he says again—a single word that makes me shudder. "That's his name. He named the stall after his wife he lost. I don't know, maybe cancer. I didn't ask." He shrugs and I feel like I'm free falling without a parachute to stop me from hitting the ground and becoming human pulp.

"Hey, miss, you okay?"

The floor tilts and wobbles as I command my feet to move. Bending down, I bring my gun to my hand and hold it just out of sight inside my blazer.

"Move…move…out the way," I snarl to the people standing between me and him.

It's him. It's him. It's him.

Macy.

The name comes into view as people part like the sea.

Doll with the Jade Eyes.

Thud…thud…thud…

There's one table, but nobody's there. A lone, undressed doll lays upon it and my heart paces to a breakneck speed. It's dark brown hair is matted and filthy. Smudges are smeared all over the doll's face. Her cloth body has been torn and stuffing hangs out.

I jerk my head around, scanning the faces and nooks in hopes of seeing him hiding. My hand skitters over the table until my fingers find the doll. Bringing it up to my eyes, I scan over it. A tag hangs around its neck.

DIRTY LITTLE DOLL.

The world expands and then closes in around me as

my fingers release the doll. It hits the grass with a *thud* and my eyes close for a moment. When I reopen them, I see him, through the crowd staring at me. It's him. Benny.

It has to be him.

I yank my arm from my jacket, the gun aiming straight out in front of me, my finger on the trigger, ready to end this—to end him.

"Benny!" I shout, moving toward him. He doesn't move. Simply stares at me through the throng of people.

It's him.

His eyes hold mine, the hollow pits of hell blazing from them as I get closer and closer.

He wants to die, because he's not moving. He's waiting for me to get closer—he's waiting for me to shoot him. Screams echo all around me and bodies blur in my peripheral as they move at an abnormal speed.

I'm so close.

He looks feral and determined. There's a smirk on his lips, like he has a secret and I'm not a part of it. He licks his lips—lips that used to know every single part of my body—as that thick, untamed curly hair of his falls over his face, and then…

"Oomph."

I'm tackled from the side and my ribs ignite in pain. My face hits the dirt and I inhale a mouthful. My chest heaves and I splutter to choke it from my mouth.

Noise roars all around me, making my ears pop. A heavy weight keeps me pinned to the earth.

"Suspect in custody," a deep voice rumbles from the chest of whoever is holding me down.

My eyes scan the space to where Benny was standing.

It's now empty. As if he was never there.

A ghost.

"Get off me. It's him," I cough. "I'm a police officer. Get off. It's him," I yell, feeling the veins bulge in my temples.

"It's him." Why is no one listening to me?

I'm cuffed and dragged to my feet. A young guy in full uniform smiles at me like he just won the big bear at the carnival. *Idiot.* I scan the people, the empty spaces—nothing.

"I'm Detective Phillips and *was* in pursuit of a very dangerous man," I hiss out, my ribs hindering me as pressure tightens around my abdomen. If he broke a freaking rib, there will be hell to pay for this idiot.

"I had him, goddammit. I had him."

"Phillips? Uncuff her now," a familiar voice barks.

Marcus. Thank God.

"The man who killed the woman in the doll shop," I wisp out. "He was here. Shut this place down. Don't let anybody leave." The world around me tilts as his face doubles. His voice distorts as the sky swirls around and…

―――

"I have a new dress for my pretty doll," he says. "Do you want to see it?"

No, I want to wear it. I'm freezing to death.

"I need a blanket, Benny," I murmur, my teeth chattering.

He tosses the dress he was fumbling with for Macy onto his table and marches over to my cell.

"Benjamin," he barks. "How many fucking times do I

have to tell you?"

"I'm freezing, Benjamin," I placate in hopes he will find mercy in his black, dead heart.

"I like it when you're cold. It turns your skin a shade paler," he muses as his eyes feast over my naked, vampire-looking skin. "Like porcelain."

"It's called death's door, Benjamin." I shiver and rub at myself, trying to keep warm.

"I can warm you up." His growled offer makes me want to die. If a tear were to leak from my eye, it would probably freeze upon my skin. The thought of his warm flesh against mine doesn't repulse me. Instead, all I can think about is feeling heat. Maybe he would leave me with his sweater after.

"Okay," I tell him, and his head snaps up to meet my eyes.

"What?"

"Okay," I repeat, stepping back from the door so he can unlock it and come inside.

Clanking sounds, and then he's inside my cell, eagerly undressing. I watch as his clothes drop to the floor, wishing I could curl up in them to steal their warmth. Walking toward him, I can already feel the heat radiating from his body. My arms go up around his neck and he stiffens briefly before relaxing. Grabbing my waist, he lifts me and I comply, wrapping my legs around him. So warm. So nice. His temperature against the cold of my flesh burns almost before it seeps into me, giving me relief from the harshness of its bite.

He backs us up and drops so he's sitting on my bed. Crushing my body to his, I writhe over him to get as much of his warmth as possible. His cock thickens and grows against the apex of my thighs and he becomes frantic, lifting me and pulling me down onto his length. We both hiss as he enters me—both feeling pleasure from two entirely different sensations. I begin to buck against him and his eyes watch me in wonder. In this moment, I don't care that I'm whoring myself to my captor to keep from freezing to death. My blood is already pumping through my veins, keeping me alive. I move my hips faster, lifting my ass up and down over him as I do. He bares down on my shoulder with his teeth and draws blood. His rough hands squeeze at my breasts too hard to give pleasure, but I don't care. He's warm.

"I'm going to come," he groans. "I'm going to fucking come."

He growls aloud and then grips me tight. His arms hold me still as his hips jut up from the bed into me, once, twice… and then his hot cum floods into my body and I know I'll be left sticky for the night. The pipes are too noisy and he hates using the taps at night.

"That was amazing," he puffs against my skin, and the nausea that always accompanies the end of a visit from Benny stirs in my gut.

I lift myself from him and crawl over the bed, curling into a ball under the flimsy sheet. His feet stomp toward the cell door and stop. I look up as he swipes up his clothes and something heavy hits the bed.

"You can wear this, but only for sleeping. If you have it on when you're not in the bed, I'll shred it and you can freeze your fucking ass off."

Nodding emphatically, I graciously take his offering. A sweater. "Okay, thank you," I tell him, sickening myself further for offering him my gratitude for a basic human right.

"I promise."

It smells of him. I now can't even escape him in my dreamless sleep.

But right now, I don't care.

I'm warm.

"Benny!"

I jerk upright and hiss in pain as my ribs protest. Dillon is quickly by my side, guiding me back into a lying position.

"Don't try to sit up," he instructs, a little too late. "You have a cracked rib. Some fucking rookie took you down."

"Why didn't you show up at eleven?" I wheeze. The light in the room is blinding. I'm in a hospital bed. The itchy blanket over my legs brings back memories of my rehabilitation after I escaped Benny. "Where were you?"

His brow furrows, guilt twisting his features. Sitting on the bed, he takes my hand in his.

"We got a call. A man had been brought in, barely breathing. Some woman said he was on the side of the road mumbling about a woman who attacked him with a crowbar."

"What?"

He nods his head and places his other hand over our joined ones. "He said you by name, Jade. Told them you forced him to pull over, showed him your badge, and made him exit his vehicle, to which you then proceeded to attack him with a crowbar."

Lines crinkle my forehead as I try to make sense of his words. "He's lying, obviously," I protest with a huff, trying to sit up again. Surely Dillon believes me.

"Don't move," he grumbles. "You'll only hurt yourself more." Dillon gently pushes against my shoulders until I relax into the mattress. "We then got a call about a madwoman waving a gun in the air calling for a Benny."

A shudder ripples through me at the mention of him. "He was there, Dillon," I mutter. "He was right there." I beg at him with my eyes.

"I believe you," he says softly. "I do…"

"But?" I hiss, studying the worry storming in his chocolate orbs.

"They found the bloody crowbar in your trunk."

My eyes pop wide open. "What? No, that's impossible. He's lying. I want to see him." I pull at a needle in my hand and ignore the blood pumping from the little hole now there.

"Jade, for fuck's sake, stop," he orders with a growl. He attempts to hold my hands still, but I struggle against him, my blood making a mess of the white sheet covering my lap. "We need a nurse in here, goddammit!"

"Let me go, Dillon," I screech. "I need to know why he's lying about what happened. Maybe whoever hit him is blackmailing him."

"You can't talk to him," he argues. "He's in the OR. Critical condition."

Hot tears well in my eyes. "I want to be left alone." I pull my arm from his grasp.

"Don't do this," he says, his tone beseeching. "Don't pull away from me. I'm trying to help you."

"Nurse," I demand when I locate the call button, and he flinches in response.

A skinny woman appears at the door and looks in at the bloody mess I've made of my hand. She groans and then hollers for another nurse to help her.

"I want to be left alone," I repeat. They both turn to look at Dillon and when he moves from the bed, I instantly mourn the loss of his comfort.

He shakes his head and rubs at the blood from my hand on his. "Don't push me away, Jade. We will get this monster and I will make you realize you're not alone in this anymore. Nothing anyone can say or claim can turn me from you or make me believe this is all in your head. And I certainly don't believe you beat a man twice your size to near death with a fucking crowbar. DNA doesn't lie which is why this stupid accusation will be thrown out before morning." He nods once and then I'm staring at his retreating back. The door swings closed behind him as he leaves and a sob rips from my chest. The pain is excruciating in my ribs, but I fight through it, letting myself cry.

CHAPTER THIRTEEN

~ *Crimson* ~

"**D**OES IT HURT?"

My hand lifts to the bruise on my cheek and I raise a nonchalant shoulder.

"It's what happens when a man tackles you."

"Who was the man?"

"What does it matter?"

She shifts in her seat and I stare at the water. Today, she's added a celery stick to it. I want to scream at her, ask why, but I don't. Instead, I gaze at it, tiny bubbles collecting in the bottom. It must have been sitting out a while.

"You appear sad today," she says. "Why is that?"

Flicking my eyes to hers, I will her to burst into a fiery ball of flames, but she doesn't.

You appear sad.

I can't believe we have to pay for this crap.

"Maybe I am sad," I offer, pinning her with my stoic stare.

"Can you tell me why that is? What's happened to make you feel this way?"

She crosses her legs and places her pen down on the arm of her chair. She's back in one of those gutsy pantsuits.

"Can I ask you a question?" I muse, leaning forward

and rubbing at a scuff on my shoe.

"Of course." She smiles, picking up her pen.

"Have you ever wanted something so badly, you envision it, but don't know whether what you're seeing is reality or just your own need for it to be real?"

She looks off into her sparse apartment, contemplating my question. "When a person has been through something traumatic, it's not unusual for them to seek a resolution in their mind. It's a coping mechanism—a way for them to finally be able to move on. You're not crazy." She smiles again.

"I didn't say I was crazy," I bite out, standing abruptly.

Placing her pad down, she leans forward, clasping her hands together. "I didn't mean to offend you."

"You suck at your job."

I leave her open-mouthed.

I've had enough of her for one day.

CHAPTER FOURTEEN

~ *Oxblood* ~

My cell phone continues to light up with Dillon's name, but I can't bring myself to answer it. I discharged myself from the hospital and have been curled up on my couch ignoring his calls. Nothing makes sense. I feel as though I'm sleepwalking through a nightmare and can't find a way to wake the hell up.

Ding.

I lift my head to see a text from Dillon, but I don't read it.

"So, you *are* alive and you *are* getting my calls." His baritone booms through my apartment, startling me. "You're just choosing to ignore me."

"Uh," I groan. "Ouch." My rib throbs in pain.

He stalks over to me and drops to his knees beside the couch. "Shit, I'm sorry." Dark brown eyebrows furl together as he assesses me for damage. When he reaches out to stroke at my hair, I swat him away.

"What the hell are you doing in here, Dillon. How did you get in?"

Reaching into his pocket, he pulls out a key. My key. "You gave it to me when I went for beer the other night."

Crap, I did do that.

"Well, this isn't the other night and it was a one-time only use," I snap, snatching it from his grasp. The movement makes me wince when my rib throbs again.

"I won't let you shut me out and yourself in, Jade. I won't do it."

"Leave me alone, Dillon."

"Right. Well, if you're going to be a brat, then we can do this the hard way." He grabs at some of my discarded clothes slung on a chair. "Get dressed. You can't leave the house like that."

I skim my gaze over my black panties, the bandage around my ribs, and a cut-off Pink Floyd tee.

"You look like an eighties cardio instructor." He smirks, and it's annoyingly cute.

"Why do I need to be dressed?" I whine, already feeling defeated. "I'm not going anywhere."

He sighs and places his hands on his hips. "Phillips, get your fucking clothes on and then down to my car. I have to take you in to see the chief."

This gets my attention and I sit up a little too quickly, causing pain to rip down my side. Oh God, he's going to fire me, or arrest me, or commit me. They can't possibly believe the asshole who said I almost beat him to death.

"Did the guy make it?"

Nodding, he runs a hand through his hair and dark circles that weren't there before are beginning to form under his eyes. He looks tired. This is what I do. I'm like a poison, polluting the people I care about.

"He's still critical, but he's going to make it. Get dressed and meet me downstairs in five."

I can't stop the bouncing of my knee. I'm nervous and don't want to be here. Everyone stalked me with their eyes across the precinct once I arrived. Holding my hands up and asking if they wanted to take a picture so it would last longer didn't go down well either. Now Dillon is glaring at me from a seat three feet from my own.

"Stop fucking bouncing your leg, Jade." He pinches the bridge of his nose with his thumb and forefinger and I fight the smile wanting to lift my lips. I like when he calls me Jade. His tough love and silent treatment I got the entire ride over here didn't last.

The office door slams shut and Chief Stanton walks past us. Once behind his desk, he drops his ass into the chair and plonks a folder on the desk before shoving it toward me.

"What's this?"

"Medical report on Adam Maine."

I grab the file and see the picture of the asshole from the flea market.

Adam Maine.

"His injuries were too substantial to have been carried out by someone of your size," he says gruffly. "Him being hit with a truck is a hell of a lot more likely."

"Just like I said," I mutter under my breath, earning a nudge of warning from Dillon's foot. I flip through the medical report. There's a bunch of jargon I don't understand sandwiched between the words that do stand out: collapsed lung, broken femur, shattered ribcage, broken breast bone, collar bone, hip bone, internal bleeding from a punctured kidney…the list goes on and on.

"How he's alive is anyone's guess," Stanton says. "The doctors are baffled, but it's good for you that he is. When he recovers, we can question him."

"So I'm cleared?" I ask. "I can come back to work?"

"I'm not going to lie, Phillips," Stanton grumbles, "you going all Mad Max at a fucking craft fair full of civilians—mostly grandmas and shit—and this whole bit with the crowbar where a half-dead guy ends up in the hospital is not the best news to come out of this precinct. It won't be the last either. However, I am going to need you to take a longer leave of absence until this case is resolved. You're too close to it. Too damn involved. So, no, you're not cleared. Not yet."

My mouth pops open, but he holds his hand up to stop me.

"Don't argue with me on this," he warns. "This is not a request."

"And me?" Dillon asks him.

Stanton leans forward on his desk, clasping his hands together. "You will work this fucking case and find out if that maniac from Phillips' past has come back to toy with her. If he has, we take this sonofabitch down."

My mind is racing.

I can't think or sit still.

All I can do is pace and pace and pace around my living room.

I'm driving Dillon bonkers.

"I can't just do nothing," I complain to a fatigued Dillon.

He scrubs his now scruffy jaw with his palm and shoots me a firm glare. "You don't have a choice in the matter right now, Jade. This fucker is out there trying to set you up. Who knows what his end game is. It's too risky," he growls. "I won't risk *you*."

I know what Benny wants.

Dirty little doll.

"I want you to promise me you're going to stay here, rest, and let me do my job."

"Fine," I huff, waving my hand in the air, defeated.

"Jade," he warns.

"I promise."

He places a kiss on my nose and leaves me. As much as I want to go after Benny, I don't have any leads. The events of the day catch up to me and I barely make it to my couch before I pass out.

I wake with a start and for the first time, I'm not shrieking when a man touches me in the dark. The rough fingertips threading into my hair are familiar. Peppermint with a hint of coffee envelops me and I recognize the scent to be Dillon's.

"What time is it?" I murmur, attempting to make out his form in the darkness.

His full lips press against mine and I part my lips, granting him access. He kisses me hard until I'm gasping for air.

"Late." His whispered answer doesn't tell me anything. He gently skims his palm over my T-shirt, cupping my breast in the process. I let out a needy moan to which he chuckles. Deep and warm. Inviting. Rubbing my thighs together, I attempt to alleviate the need throbbing for him at my core.

"Anything new I should know about?"

Dillon clocks out at five, if at all possible. The fact that he's here hours later tells me something came up.

"I don't want to talk about it," he growls.

His voice, despite the bite, seems shaken. Something upset the unflappable Dillon Scott. Pushing his shoulders, I sit up, making out his shadowed form kneeling beside the couch.

"Tell me," I demand.

The shadow stands and stalks out of my living room. With a grunt, I hop up and run after him toward my bedroom. My side aches from my cracked rib, but it doesn't deter me. Light pours from my room and when I make it inside, he's flicking through the buttons of his dress shirt, a scowl on his face.

"I have to shower," he snaps before ripping off his shirt.

My eyes skim over his tanned flesh. He peels off his white undershirt and once again dazzles me with his sculpted form. For someone who eats doughnuts like they're going damned extinct, he sure looks mighty good. He probably has to work extra hard because of his sugar obsession. I'm still gaping at his body when he shoves his slacks down along with his boxers. His butt is cute and tight. I want to bite it.

When he turns to look at me, all the lust drains away. His brown eyes are heavy with sadness. His forehead is marred with lines. He looks broken. Devastated. Without thinking, I launch myself into his arms, ignoring his thick cock between us.

"What happened?" I implore, my voice pleading for answers.

He strokes my messy hair and kisses the top of my head. "Too much, baby. Too fucking much." While my heart does a little patter and warms at his endearment, my skin grows cold.

"Was it related to Benny?"

His entire body tenses. I don't need him to verbally answer because he already did. Something happened.

"Tell me."

He jerks out of my grip and stalks into my bathroom like he owns the place, his back muscles rippling with every step he takes. I quite like how his massive frame fills my tiny bathroom.

"Dillon…"

A shudder ripples through him as he turns on the water. He doesn't even wait for it to warm before he steps into the icy spray, a hiss leaving his lips.

Annoyed at being ignored, I peel off my T-shirt and bra. Once I shove my panties and jeans to the floor, I slip into the still cool shower beside him and chew on my bottom lip, waiting for him to speak. The water heats up quickly and soon, steam billows around us. His back is turned from me, so I rest my forehead against his hard flesh and hug him from behind.

"She looked like you…"

I freeze at his words. "Who?" *Please don't tell me my sister is dead.*

"Jane Doe."

"Is it Macy?" I breathe into the mist, willing it to evaporate me into it.

"No. I had Jesse in the lab check her blood straightaway. He owed me a favor. It wasn't her, I promise."

Splaying my palms on his hard, lower torso, I give a silent prayer of thanks to God, but the shame coats me in its grime. She was someone's sister, daughter, friend, child.

"What happened to the vic?"

A deep, ragged breath escapes him. "She was so dirty."

Dirty little doll.

I swallow down the bile in my throat. "Is she?"

"Yes, a homicide, baby."

Baby.

I let the word comfort me even though I'm about to throw up. "Where?"

"Sixteen miles from town. Naked. Lacerations all over her."

"Sounds like Benny." My voice is a whisper.

Benny.

Dillon twists in my grip and threads his fingers into my half-wet hair. "Her face was so pretty. Not a cut or bruise or anything. She had these long fucking fake eyelashes on. Blush had been smeared heavily on her cheeks. And her lips were painted blood red."

I shudder just thinking of how Benny would dress up Macy. He never let me see her, but I saw him dragging his cart into her cell. A cart full of makeup and wigs and such. And all those stupid frilly dresses he'd spend hours sewing for her to wear.

Dillon's eyes narrow as fear flickers in his dark orbs.

"Jade," he murmurs, his thumbs rubbing circles on my temples, "I'm so sorry."

"Sorry for what?"

"That the fucker did that shit to you!" he roars, every muscle in his body flexing with rage. "She'd been sexually assaulted, Jade. Late teens and this girl was raped, mutilated, and left on the side of the road like she didn't fucking matter. She fucking mattered! *You* fucking matter!"

His mouth crashes to mine and he kisses me with desperation. A low moan escapes me when his palm slips under my thigh. Without effort, he lifts me and my legs automatically wrap around his solid waist. Our tongues tease and torment each other as his hardened cock slides between us. My rib aches, but he's not hurting me—no, everything he's doing to my body feels really damn good.

"Fuck me, Dillon," I murmur against his mouth. "Take it all away, just for a moment."

He grunts his agreement and then I can feel the tip of his smooth cock pressing at my center. Dillon is bigger than any man I've been with, but with the water sluicing between us, he easily slides into my wet, needy body.

God, he's so big.

Every part of me stretches, filling with him.

"Jesus fucking Christ," he hisses as he backs me up against the tile. His palms grip my ass, keeping me suspended in the air as he brutally drives into me. I hold onto his neck for dear life as he pounds into me.

Everything with Benny was so wrong, yet at times, it felt twistedly right.

Everything with Bo was so right, but most times, it felt horribly wrong.

But with Dillon?

He feels unbelievably right. Nothing wrong at all about what he's doing to my body.

The connection between us as he grinds into me is electric. It burns and sizzles in the atmosphere around us, cocooning us in this sexually charged bubble no one can touch. We're safe in here and the world isn't a horrible place because in this moment, nothing and no one but the two of us exist.

"Touch your pussy, Jade. I've been stroking off to the thought of you for months. Now that I finally have you, I won't last long. I want you coming on my cock when I come. Hear me, baby?" he demands, his fingers digging into my ass cheeks.

"Y-Yes," I tell him as I slip my hand between us. With him stretching me wide and my fingertips on my clit, I go insane with pleasure. My entire body thrums with the need to orgasm.

"That's my girl," he grunts as he bucks into me. "Rub that clit hard."

I quicken my pace until my nerves light on fire.

"Oh God," I gasp, the fingernails on my free hand digging into his neck.

So close.

So, so close.

"I'm going to come, goddammit!" he curses, and then bites on my bottom lip. Not hard enough to draw blood, just enough to leave his delicious mark.

A burst of heat surges into me. That, coupled with the way he verges on the edge of painful yet pleasurable and how I'm massaging myself, sends me into a fit of quakes raging through my body. Stars glitter in my vision and for a few brief moments, I'm lost to the sublime sensations.

"Dillon," I gasp, my entire body still rippling with pleasure. "Dillon."

He buries his nose into my wet hair in search of my earlobe. When his hot breath tickles me there, I let out a small giggle. It makes me clench around his softening cock.

"That was…"

He nips at my neck just below my ear. "Fucking fantastic?"

Laughing, I nod. "Who knew you had it in you, Detective?"

His cock begins to harden again, but much to my disappointment, he slips out of me and sets me on my shaking feet. "Did I hurt your rib?" Dark, caring eyes caress my flesh as he assesses me.

"I'm fine," I tell him with a smile.

He flashes me a crooked grin before it falls away. "Shit," he groans, running his fingers through his wet, messy hair hanging in his eyes. "I'm sorry, I should have checked with you first. Tell me you're on the pill?"

Sadness saturates every part of my flesh, muscles, bones, and finally my soul. "Don't worry, I can't get pregnant. Not after all the trauma I suffered from Benny."

His face becomes murderous. Red. Contorted in rage. *Mine.*

A sense of possessiveness washes over me. Dillon is different. He understands my past and my desire to seek revenge. Nobody has ever gotten inside me like he does. Poor Bo tried, but he would only get so far before my walls were up. With Dillon, my walls never stood a chance.

I slide my palms to his scruffy cheeks. "We're going to get him back and make him pay. You promised, remember?"

His mouth crashes to mine.

Again, I don't need a verbal answer.

This kiss tells me everything I already know.

We're going to make Benny pay.

"Eat," he orders as he sets a plate of pizza rolls on my nightstand.

I lift my gaze from my laptop and peruse his nearly naked body. After our shower earlier, he fucked me again on my bed. This time, softer and sweeter. Not Bo sweet. Different. Better. Addicting. *Lovemaking.*

"Fifteen miles from her dorm. How do you think she got there?" I question as I take one of the steaming hot pizza rolls and blow on it. Dillon received a text a little while ago from Stanton stating the vic is no longer a Jane Doe. Silvia Collins, age twenty, college kid.

He sheds his boxers and climbs into bed beside me. Once he pulls the sheet over his impressive flaccid cock, he looks at the map I have pulled up. I've pinned the location of her dorm and also the location where she was found.

Same place Adam Maine got plowed by a truck right in front of me.

Same place I was plowed by a truck eight years ago.

There's no denying this is Benny's work. I know this. Dillon knows this. Even Chief Stanton knows this.

"Maybe he lured her into the van like he did you and Macy?" he suggests.

I hand him my pizza roll and zoom out on the screen. "You said her feet were torn to shreds, right?"

He nods. "Consistent with running."

"I ran hard that night. Terrified for my life. Everything was a blur. I stepped on rocks and thorns and prickly bushes. None of it mattered or slowed me. Adrenaline drove me on," I say, mostly to myself.

He sits up and turns to look at me. "How far did they estimate you ran?"

"Based on my dehydrated and abused state, they said it was about four miles max. They ended up expanding the search area another two miles in diameter just in case," I tell him absently.

Dillon steals my laptop and pulls up Google. He searches the vic's name and finds loads of articles from her running track at her college.

"What was your best time at the academy for a mile?"

Frowning, I shrug my shoulders. "The day I was tested it was just under seven, but I'd been clocking six and a half minute miles in training. I'd been on my period that day. It was a struggle to even make that time."

He pulls up a calculator and starts inputting some figures. "Silvia's best time was just under six minutes. But barefoot..." he pinches the bridge of his nose as he thinks, "I'm thinking it could have made it closer to eight. However, add in adrenaline, and she's back under seven, give or take."

"Yeah?"

He lets out a ragged sigh. "She was last seen at her

dorm just as it was getting dark. Eight forty-five or so. Her roommate said she was dressed for a run, but then," he pauses, clutching my hand, "they found her shoes in the parking lot."

"You think Benny chased her? There's no way he'd let her win. He'd mow her down with his dumb van," I argue.

Dillon leans across me, his body heat burning my flesh, steals more pizza rolls, and forces two of them into my palm.

"What if he wanted her to run? To send you a message?"

My blood runs cold in my veins. "You think he chased her on purpose? Surely someone at the college would have seen."

"Not if he abducted her, took her away from campus, and then let her go. Not if he took her someplace and did all those things to her first. Between the campus and the spot her body was found, there's a shitty motel. What if he took her there first?" he ponders aloud.

"We need to check that motel."

"I'll text Jefferson and have him investigate," he assures me.

"What's the distance between the motel and where they found her?" My brain hurts, but I'm hell-bent on figuring this out.

He runs his fingers through his dark brown hair and tugs at it. "Look it up. Has to be at least ten miles."

I take the laptop and check the distance.

"Thirteen miles," we both say at once.

"So, you're scared, running for your life," he says quickly, "but you're barefoot, naked, and injured. Just like you were. A normal runner could make that time quickly, but her scenario wasn't normal. The adrenaline, though, kicks up your speed a bit. So you'd basically be close to your best time anyway."

"Approximately ninety minutes she ran along that dark stretch of highway with him chasing her?" I question, a shiver coursing through me just thinking about the terror that girl faced.

"Give or take. It lines up with the approximate time of death, which would have occurred right around the time she made it to that spot," he tells me. "He wanted her to run that distance from him. Probably chased her with his vehicle. When she got where he wanted her, he dispatched her."

His eyes find mine, questions dancing in them.

"What are you thinking?" I ask.

"How long did you tell them you ran for?" he inquires before shoving a pizza roll into his mouth. I'm still holding the two he gave me in my palm.

"I didn't know. Told them it seemed like hours. By the time I came to three weeks later, they'd already canvassed a six-mile radius in search of my sister. They found nothing. And when I told them to search farther, they kindly explained it wasn't possible in my condition. Six miles was stretching it."

Tugging one of the pizza rolls from my hand, he makes me eat it, and then the other one before he speaks again.

"What if you ran farther than those six miles? What if he's leaving a clue so you'll come find him?" His brows furl together, as if the very notion pisses him off.

"He clearly left that clue on the craft fair's website. Just a small detail to get me out there on my own. When I got to that booth, there was just the single abused doll with the message on it. I think he probably would have tried to lure me away from the crowd and taken me again had Officer Douche not gone all psycho football player on me."

Dillon's features harden. "What was the message on the doll you said he left you? It was missing when they went back to check the scene."

DIRTY LITTLE DOLL.

My throat constricts and I choke out the words. "It's what he used to call me…"

"Dirty little doll," he says with a low growl. Even though it's spoken by Dillon and not Benny, it still sends a ripple of terror quivering through me. His arm wraps around me and he pulls me against his side. "It was carved along the homicide vic's upper chest post mortem." He lets out a furious hiss. "I'm going to slice that motherfucker from his throat to his dick and let you rip his goddamned insides out."

CHAPTER FIFTEEN

~ Wine ~

"You're going to stay here with your doors locked at all times. Shoot any motherfucker who dares enter unless it's me, of course," Dillon says with a smirk, the steam from his coffee billowing around his face.

He looks sexy as hell today in a pair of black slacks and a fitted pale blue button-up shirt. Because it's hotter than hades outside, he's already rolled his sleeves up to his elbows. The muscles in his forearms ripple with each movement. The veins are plentiful and prominent—just like his cock. And I should know, I got a close up encounter from my knees in the middle of the night.

Despite the horrors around me, I'm oddly satisfied Dillon and I have grown closer. It takes the edge off the ever-present stress. I've actually enjoyed myself while with him. Even though we've been working together to find Benny and Macy, he's also distracted me. We're able to turn all that off the moment his body joins with mine. I've never had a safe haven before…it's always been Benny stuck inside my head twenty-four seven.

Dillon drives him away.

Dillon fills that space with his intense, intoxicating presence.

Dillon is the ultimate distraction and I welcome it wholeheartedly.

Benny, for once, can't win. Dillon is the alpha male who beats on his chest and dominates my headspace.

"You know I won't hesitate to shoot him if he comes into my home," I assure him.

His eyes drag over my body. Since I don't have to work, I'm just wearing a loose white tank top and pair of lacey pink panties. I like that he's so affected by me. In all the months we've worked together, he never once let on he'd been interested.

"When they finally let you come back to work, it's going to be hard as fuck not to bend you over your desk and take you from behind," he says with a growl while setting his mug down on the counter.

I laugh as he prowls over to me. My body is sore from yesterday, but he doesn't hurt me in his embrace. His nose nuzzles into my hair and he inhales me.

"God," he grumbles, "your scent is going to be the death of me. How the hell am I supposed to focus today with you clinging to my skin?"

His mouth finds mine and he kisses me hard and eager with a hunger that seems to consume him. My palms roam his chest until I grip his erection through his pants. The man is insatiable. He fucked me raw last night and I'm still sore, but somehow, I'm growing wet just thinking about his cock inside me.

"I have to leave," he complains before his mouth devours mine. He doesn't seem in any hurry. My shirt is all but torn from my body and I let out a yelp when he slides down to suckle my collarbone. Then his mouth is on my nipple, sucking and biting and pulling with his teeth. My nipples are on fire from his constant abuse, yet they're erect, eager for more. His hair is freshly gelled and I'm dying to mess it back up. My fingers thread into his hair and I yank enough to make him groan.

"Fuck," he murmurs, his hands finding my panties. Hastily, he shoves them down my thighs and twists me away from him. "Bend over, baby."

Baby.

A ripple of excitement washes over me.

Turning away, I lean over the island and his large palm smacks my ass, causing me to squeal.

"Ugh!" I shriek. "Asshole."

Then his belt is jingling, his fingers are parting me open, and that fat cock of his is inside me in one hard thrust.

"Oh God!" I cry out, my fingers clawing at the countertop.

The sound of his flesh slapping against mine echoes in the kitchen. He takes me brutally from behind, but his fingers roam my back, gently caressing. Dillon fucks me like a lion would his bitch in heat as his protectiveness washes over me.

This pain mixed with pleasure…Dillon gives me what Bo never could.

His thumb and finger pinch my clit, jolting me back to the moment. A few seconds more of his delicious, torturous assault and I'm coming hard on his cock. He fists his fingers in my messy hair and slightly yanks as he fills me with his release. The groan that escapes him is hot and nearly has me begging him to take me back to my room for round two this morning.

"You're going to get my ass fired," he complains as he pulls out of me. His hot cum runs down my inner thigh to my knee. Another pop on my ass has me jerking my head over my shoulder to glare at him. But as soon as I see his disheveled hair and shit-eating grin, I'm done for. He's made me weak for him. For once in my entire terrible life, I actually like feeling weak.

"Call in sick," I tease as I slide my panties up my wet thighs. "I could take care of you."

He tucks his dripping cock into his boxers and yanks his slacks up. While he fastens his pants, he shakes his head at me. "Who knew you were such a vixen, Jade? Had I known we would have been this good together, I'd have fucked you in the back of the Crown Vic the first day we were assigned together. I didn't realize your bitchiness was how you flirted."

Laughing, I swat at him. "You're an ass."

His fingers bite into my hips as he hauls me to him. Those perfect full lips press against mine and he kisses me hard. Every time with Dillon is rough and needy and raw. I've never experienced anything like it.

When he finally breaks away from our breathtaking kiss, he levels me with a serious gaze. "Don't leave at all today," he instructs. "Promise me you'll be here naked and waiting by the time I get back home."

The tingling up my spine and bruise I feel throbbing at my lips from his passion has me in a state of intoxication that's threefold when he calls my place his home. I'm still reeling that I don't even register the quick kiss to my lips and then the slam of the front door several moments later.

Home.

Dillon feels like the closest thing.

I've been researching areas farther than the six-mile radius I originally obsessed over for hours. Lunch has come and gone with no word from my partner. By Dillon's calculations, I could have been farther out, so I double it and start checking properties within a twelve-mile radius. I'm buried in details when my phone starts to ring.

"Hello?" I answer, my mind absent as I scroll along the screen.

"Hello to you, too," a deep, familiar voice growls, "dirty little doll."

My blood turns to ice and the caller—fucking Benny—now has my undivided attention. "Where is my sister?" I demand, switching my phone to speaker so I can look for a number. Thank God there is one. "Where the fuck is she, asshole?"

He chuckles, the tone dark and sinister, just like I remember. My entire body quakes with fear. It's been years since I last heard his voice, but it feels like only yesterday.

"After you abandoned her—abandoned us both—do you even care? It's not her you need to worry about anyway," he spits out. "You need to worry about that motherfucker."

Dillon.

Pain slices through me at the thought of Benny hurting him too. "No!"

"Yes…"

Bingo. Gas station seven miles from here. He's so close. Shit!

"If you hurt him, I swear to God, I'll kill you, Benny!" I threaten.

"Benjamin," he seethes. "You call me Benjamin."

Ignoring him and pulling up my inbox, I start typing an email to the entire department.

Murder and kidnapping suspect known as Benjamin AKA Benny called my cell. Reverse search says phone call is coming from a payphone at the Stop N Save on the corner of Delaware and Hollister. I'm in pursuit now. Send back up immediately!

I hit send and shove my feet into my shoes. "I'm no longer playing your games, Benny. You're going to give me my sister and turn yourself in to the authorities."

He's not stupid. I just want to keep him talking. The longer he stays on the phone, the better chance I have of arresting him. With my Glock in my hip holster, I bolt out the front door and jog toward my car.

"We both know I'm not going to turn myself in," he says smugly. "Do you miss me, pretty little doll? Do you miss the way I fucked your tight cunt while you screamed and begged for someone to save you? Do you remember the way you used to come so hard when my mouth was on your pussy? Such a dirty, dirty doll. Why did you run away from me—from us? I kept her just for you and that was how you showed me your appreciation?"

Bile rises in my throat, but I choke it down. "You're a monster. You better pray my sister is still alive and well. If you did anything to her, I will cut your heart out and feed it to you."

"You're so dramatic. Always were a feisty one. There's no other who compares to you, " he tells me, his voice low. "Always wanting to be the star of the show. Always wanting me to fuck you instead of her. Such a jealous doll, weren't you?"

"Fuck you!" I snarl as I speed down the road, my lights on but siren off.

My phone beeps, but I don't try to answer it. I have to keep his ass on the line.

"You already did, dirty doll, you even asked for it at times. I fucked you many times and God, did it feel good. I haven't felt anything like it since the day you ran out on me. Truth is, you're my favorite doll," he says, a sick smile in his voice. "And I want you fucking back!" His roar causes me to shriek and nearly drop the phone. A terrified sob sticks in my throat, but I swallow it down.

"I'm not coming back," I hiss, desperately trying to keep the wobble out of my voice.

"Don't you miss her?"

Tears well in my eyes and I blink them away quickly so I can see the road. "So much." A whisper is all I can manage.

"What about him? Do you miss him?" There's a jealous bite to his tone. How he knows about Dillon and me is surprising. What if he's been in my home?

"I don't know what you're talking about," I snap.

He barks out a laugh. "Are you not curious how I got your phone number? Your little boyfriend. I keep waiting for you to call him, but you don't. Seems he's as disposable to you as we were—I was. I suppose I hurt him for no reason then."

"What have you done?"

The line is silent a moment and I fear he's hung up. Finally, he breathes heavily into the receiver. "I needed a boy doll to add to my collection."

A tear streaks down my cheek.

I'm poison.

This dark cloud called Benny follows me wherever I go, wreaking havoc on the lives in my world.

"Let him go…"

"He shouldn't have preyed on you when you were a little girl. I remember that picture with his scrawny arm slung over your shoulder like he owned you. Sick fuck," he seethes.

All thoughts of Dillon dissipate.

Bo.

No!

"I bet he couldn't wait to swoop in and prey on your loneliness," he snarls. "Did you miss me? I missed you."

"Don't hurt him. Benny, please."

"*Benjamin! Benjamin! Benjamin!*"

"I'm sorry," I choke in defeat, once again back to the broken doll he made me.

"Not yet, but you will be."

"Please, Benjamin."

"Goodbye, dirty little doll," he growls. "I'll be coming for you soon."

When I pull into the Stop N Save parking lot not even five minutes later, I know it's too late. He's gone. I clamber out of my vehicle with my gun raised and run to the payphone. Hot tears roll from my eyes as I let out a sob of defeat. There's a burner phone propped up on loud speaker with the payphone next to it.

He wasn't here the whole time we spoke. I never had a chance at getting here in time to catch him.

Bastard.

Bo.

I'm still standing guard, protecting my crime scene, when three squad cars and Dillon's unmarked Crown Vic squeal into the parking lot.

"There," I point at the payphone, my entire body shaking. "Check for prints and then find the bastard in the system."

Two strong arms pull me against a solid chest and I collapse as he holds me tight.

"Shhh," he murmurs into my hair. "I have you. You're safe now."

Our colleagues process the scene while Dillon coaxes information out of me. I relay the entire conversation, detail by detail. When I finish and meet his gaze, he's frowning.

"Baby…" he trails off.

Even now, stressed to the max, his word soothes me. "What?"

He closes his eyes for a moment before meeting me with a sad gaze. "The woman, the witnesses at the hospital from the hit-and-run vic…she described a black truck. Even remembered part of the license plate and gave it to the staff at the hospital. It didn't take long to see who the truck belonged to." He swallows hard.

"And?"

"Did you recognize it at all?" His brow is furrowed and he's holding onto me like I'm about to crumble.

I am.

"Uh, it happened too fast," I say, my voice hoarse. "I was in shock. The truck was too far ahead by the time I gave chase. Why?"

"Bo. Jade, the truck is registered to your ex fiancé, Bo." His groan is one of frustration. "Unless he hit him and hasn't come forward yet, it's looking likely that Benny really does have him. I'm so sorry."

CHAPTER SIXTEEN

~ *Cerise* ~

CRUISERS LINE THE DIRT ROAD leading up to Bo's and my parents' house. A frantic Maureen is holding her ankle biter dog and shaking her head. When she sees me coming, she rushes over to me, dropping the puppy to the grass.

She pulls me in for a hug, even though I don't think she's ever really approved of Bo and me. I was too damaged for her liking of a daughter-in-law.

"What's going on, Jade?" she questions, wrinkles of worry marring her forehead. "Where's Bo?"

Her new pup licks at Dillon's boot and he frowns down at it.

"When was the last time you saw Bo, Maureen?" I question.

She shakes her head and shrugs her shoulders. "I haven't seen him for weeks, but that's not unusual. He spends all his time with you or at work."

She doesn't know we broke up.

Shit.

So, he never came here?

"The work colleague," Dillon mumbles in my ear.

"And he sent that nice man here with my present."

Both Dillon and I freeze. "What present?"

She points down to the puppy, now hiking a leg up to pee on Dillon's boot. He shoos it away before it can, but it doesn't want to go. Bending down, I grasp the fur ball and lift him. His tongue snakes out and licks at my face.

"Hey, little guy."

"Who was the man? Can you walk me through what happened?" Dillon asks her, coming to stand in front of her, partially blocking me. She holds her face, anxiety building in her features.

"He was handsome with unruly hair and mesmerizing eyes," she reveals. "He said the puppy was a gift from my Bo."

The puppy's collar has a dangling nametag that catches my eye.

"Dillon," I breathe.

He glances at me over his shoulder and I hold the tag up for him to see.

DOLLY.

"Bo knows how hard it was on us when our old dog, Toby, passed away," she tells us sadly, but then furrows her brows at me. "Jade, what is it? What's going on? Where is my Bo?"

"Did you name him?" I gesture to the puppy.

Her eyes narrow as she watches someone behind me. "Why are there people looking around my property? I don't understand."

"Maureen, please listen to me," I bark out. "Can you tell me if you named the puppy?"

"No, it's a girl. She came with the nametag. I thought it was a little insensitive of Bo with everything that went on with you and your poor sister, but…" she trails off.

My head spins as vomit threatens to spill.

"He said you sent a gift for your parents also. I haven't seen them, though…"

The world around me dips and then expands.

No.

"Jade," Dillon warns, but it's too late. My body is working on its own accord. Dropping the puppy to his feet, I take off running.

"Jade!" Dillon's voice booms. Everything seems to drag into slow motion around me as I sprint toward the small house ten yards to the left.

"Jade! Stop her! Someone grab her!"

I dart past the hands reaching out for me and ignore the humming of activity behind me.

Thud.

Thud.

Thud.

Reaching the door, I skid to a halt and just stand there, gasping for air. My ribs protest the run, but the pain is irrelevant. I grab for the door handle and it gives under my weight.

No.

Pushing it open, I hear footfalls behind me.

"Everyone back off, back off," Dillon warns as his heat blasts over me from behind.

"Please, let me go in, Jade."

"I need to know they're okay. They have to be," I tell him, but I don't recognize my own voice. It's distorted, deep and broken.

"I can do that," he says with a crack in his voice. "Let

me do that for you." His hands come down on my shoulders, but I shrug him off and step inside. The scent of lilies that always hits you in the face when you first walk into my parents' home doesn't fill my senses. Instead, a stomach churning scent hits me and makes me retch.

"Jade," Dillon mutters again, his voice pained.

Every movie tells you a dead body stinks of the worst cesspool you can imagine, but the truth is, it's a distinct, weird smell—chemicals and decomposed fruit. It's not pleasant; it's harsh and potent and the very thought of what it is you're inhaling into your nose cavity is sickening.

My feet tread small steps into the living space.

Thud.

Thud.

Thud.

My dad's chair comes into view. It's positioned to face the TV—the way it always has been. The television flickers with the news channel, but there's no sound and something is written in blood red on the screen.

MONSTERS ARE HERE!

"Daddy," I weep, tears building and falling from my eyes as I step closer.

My heart thunders over the sound of Dillon trying to get me to stop from going any farther, but it's like my mind has to see—has to know this is real.

My hand shakes as I reach and touch the fabric of the chair. I spin and the weight hinders it.

"Jade, baby, please."

Stepping around the chair, my entire world crashes down around me. I collapse to the floor with a fragmented wail. "No! Oh God, no!"

He's so blue. I reach for his hand, but snatch it back when the cold ice of death's sting ignites up my fingertips. "He took his eyes," I choke. There are two bloody holes where his hazel eyes should be and a crimson river from the wound on his neck.

"Where's Mom?" I hiss into the putrid air. Clambering to my feet, I begin to search frantically.

"M-Mom…Mom…Mommy?"

I push door after door open until I stop at her bedroom.

After I shove through the door, my eyes automatically close in an effort to remove the image from my sight forever. Instead, I think it burns into my soul for eternity. I pop my eyes back open and survey what that monster did to her.

Dressed like one of Benny's dolls, Mom sits upright on the bed, her arms splayed wide, limp wrists sliced open, and the veins attached like strings on the bed post.

"Motherfucker!" Dillon hisses from behind me.

"He made his very own marionette doll," I breathe.

"Come on," he growls, "I'm getting you out of here."

Nothing feels real, like I'm touching the ground but there's no gravity keeping me bound to it. I'm floating, numb, and in a state of disbelief.

"Detective Scott!" a deep voice barks somewhere in the house for my partner, but it's disjointed and distant.

Dillon drags me back through the house. Maureen is hollering my name and then that puppy rushes into the house, wagging its tail.

"Someone get that dog!" Dillon roars. "Everyone else

stay out and call forensics. This is a crime scene." He attempts to hold me together in his strong arms and the moment he lets go, I know I'll come apart completely.

My eyes zero in on the stupid puppy. *Stop...stop...* "Stop it...STOP IT!" I scream as it laps at the blood at my dad's feet.

Dillon scoops up the dog and I run from the house, pushing past the gathering crowd of agents and neighbors. I empty the contents of my stomach with violent heaves onto the green lawn Daddy was so proud of.

"He's escalating rapidly, evolving," Detective Jefferson states, scratching his beard. "He doesn't have any victims over the age of twenty-three and the last vic was raped. That's new."

"What?" I croak, standing straight and wiping the sick from my lips with the back of my hand.

Jefferson looks at me with drawn in brows and a down-turned lip. "I'm sorry for your loss, Phillips."

"No," I hiss, "go back to what you just said. Rape is new for him?"

"There were no signs of sexual assault on the other victims." He places his hands on his hips and tilts his head.

"*I* was a victim, and he *raped* me...over and fucking over again."

"Jade," Dillon says my name again and I'm sick of hearing it. His arm reaches for me, but I shrug away from him.

"Rape isn't something new for him," I snap. "Murder and butchery isn't something new for him. These victims are older because it's a message for me. This is all for me."

"I just meant he didn't rape the other women..."

"Well he raped *me!*" I screech, causing a chorus of gasps.

I wave at them all. "Don't act like you don't already know my fucking history. Don't act like you don't all talk about it behind my back."

A rage-filled scream escapes me before I'm picked up and slung over Dillon's shoulder. I don't fight him, I just sob into his back.

My ass is placed in the passenger seat of his Crown Vic and the door is slammed shut, trapping me inside with my emotions in chaos. I'm suffocating under the weight of my reality. My heart is bleeding out and I can't patch the wound.

I gasp for air as my chest restricts, tightening. I can't breathe.

"It's okay," he coos. "It's okay." The door slams as Dillon gets in on the driver's side. His arms grip mine and I'm dragged into his lap. Straddling him, I cling to him. "Breathe. Feel my heart beat against yours." He begins tapping, *du-dum...du-dum...du-dum...*

Air washes into me and I let him bring me back to him.

"I need you inside me," I tell him.

"You're in shock, baby."

"Please, I need to feel you," I tell him, tugging at his belt buckle. He grips my wrists and then rests his head against my forehead, breathing deeply.

"There are people everywhere, baby, and you're in shock. I'm not taking you like this."

Dropping his buckle, I shake out of his hold and climb back into my own seat.

"Jade…"

"Stop," I choke out. "Just…don't say anything." My throat aches from sadness, my head roars and compresses.

"Scott, two nineteen." The crackle of the radio and beep gives us both a reprieve.

"Dispatch, this is Scott, two nineteen," he barks. "Go ahead."

"We have a match on the black truck, license plate 764 KNY."

"Go ahead," Dillon tells her, looking over at me.

"The truck has been reported as suspicious by the staff at the Six Mile Motel."

"Copy that."

He looks over at me and I can sense he doesn't want me to go before he even tells me. He's out of his mind if he thinks I'm staying here.

Knuckles rap at my window and I startle. Winding it down, I see Maureen standing there with her fucking blood-eating Dolly—a gift from a fucking psychopath.

"Jade," she questions, huge tears in her eyes. "Where's Bo?"

Shit.

"Maureen, Bo is going to be okay. I promise."

Big fat liar.

"Rename your dog." I roll the window up and order Dillon to drive.

We drive in silence and I try to blink away the vision of my parents from my mind. Gravel crunches beneath the tires as we pull onto the weathered road that leads to the cheap motel.

"There." Dillon points to the black truck.

It's Bo's.

Unclipping my belt, I push open the door and take a timid step outside.

"You don't need to be here, Jade," Dillon tells me across the roof of the car.

"Yes, I do."

We make our way over to the truck and without touching it, we look through the window into the front seat. Empty water bottles litter the floorboard in the passenger side, which is common for Bo. He's messier than the college kids he taught.

"There's blood," Dillon announces, looking into the back of the truck. A man approaches and lifts his shirt with a name badge on it.

"Hey, I'm Tim, the manager here." He nods his head and then folds his arms, rubbing the goatee on his chin.

"Can you tell us how long this truck has been parked here?" Dillon asks him.

"A couple days. We just assumed it belonged to one of our guests, but then it didn't move and we noticed the blood."

My eyes scan the area and I gesture to the camera with my head. "Does that work?"

"Yeah, they're new, but no one mans them. They upload onto the cloud." He shrugs.

So, he didn't think to go look to see who parked the truck here? I shake off my irritation and push him toward the entrance of the motel. "We're going to need to see them."

I leave Dillon to call it in and follow the willowy guy inside. It stinks of sweat and cum and if the tissues overflowing his trashcan are any indication, I'd say he uses this office as he would his bedroom.

"You're pretty for a cop."

Pretty little doll.

"I'm a detective."

"How old are you?"

Is he serious? I look like shit from crying and I'm here investigating a truck bloodied up with a woman's life splayed all over it.

"Just show me the feed, Tim," I grit out.

He pats the chair next to him.

"I'll stand."

The time stamp flickers in the corner of the screen and then the truck appears, pulling in.

Thud.

Thud.

Thud.

The truck stops and a figure gets out and walks around in direct view of the cameras. He smirks up at it, like he knows I'll be watching and holds something up in his hand.

"It's a keycard," Tim chimes.

I can see that, Tim. Like I need him narrating. *Dipshit.*

He moves across the lot and uses the key on one of the doors.

"Find out who's name that room is in," I bark at Tim, who scurries to the front desk.

I use the computer mouse to fast forward until he comes back out of the room, two hours and twelve minutes later.

"Cindy Harris," Tim blurts.

Bo's co-worker.

I watch the powerful walk of the man who kept me locked away for all those years—the man who butchered my parents. He holds up the keycard again and slips it on top of the wheel of the truck. Darting from the office and through the reception out the doors, I run over to the truck and search the tire. Just like in the video, it brushes against my fingers right where he left it.

"What's that?" Dillon asks with a firm nod. I hold the key up and point to room five with an outstretched arm.

He holds his hand out for me to give him the key and I hesitate before dropping it in his palm. I don't know if I can cope with what's behind that door. My mom's body strung up like she was a fucking doll flashes in my mind and I have to hold back the sob tearing up my chest for escape.

Dillon's heavy boots pound against the ground with my timid steps following behind. Holstering his gun, he warns me to stay back and bangs his knuckles on the door with heavy raps. "This is the police. If anyone is inside, I need you to come out slowly with your hands raised high in the air where we can see them."

Silence.

Pushing the key card into the lock, the handle gives and he gently pushes it open with his gun aimed and ready. "Jesus fuck!" he grits out, lowering his weapon and shaking his head. I come up behind him and look inside. Written on the wall in blood above the bed where a slain female lays naked are words that haunt me.

Miss Polly had a dolly who was sick, sick, sick.
So she phoned for the doctor to be quick, quick, quick.
The doctor came with his bag and his hat,
And he knocked at the door with a rat-a-tat-tat.
He looked at the dolly and shook his head,
And he said, "Miss Polly, put her straight to bed!"
He wrote on a paper for a pill, pill, pill,
"I'll be back in the morning, yes I will, will, will."

My cell buzzes in my pocket and I slip it out while waving for the people who have gathered to stand back. "Phillips," I snap into the cell.

"Did you like your gift?"

Ice floods my system, solidifying me and rooting me into the ground. "You bastard," I hiss.

"Oh, please. I did you a favor," Benny says with a click of his tongue. "Did you know your precious Bo was fucking that whore?"

"She was innocent," I bite out.

"There's no such thing," he snarls. "She was a dirty little whore. How could he ever go to her when he had you?"

"You're an animal," I choke. "You…my parents—"

"Would still be here if you didn't fucking run."

They're gone because of me.

I ran, ran, ran.

"Why now, Benny?" I scream. "Why wait all this time?"

Dillon is in my face, attempting to steal my phone, but I duck away from him.

"Benjamin," he snarls. "And every time you call me

Benny, I'm going to cut a slice out of Bo."

No.

"Why now, Benjamin?" My arm wraps around my middle and I try to stop myself from falling into the abyss of Benny's insanity while focusing on Dillon barking out orders on his cell.

"I was curious about what you would do, I suppose, and coming for you wouldn't have been easy. So I tried to get by without you." He breathes heavily into the line. "But I couldn't. They weren't you."

Thud.

Thud.

Thud.

"Who weren't? There've been no other bodies," I say aloud.

Dillon is circling me like a shark now, his hands on his hips and a firm glare on his face.

"Hmmm. Are you ready to come home now, dirty doll?"

I choke down the bile rising in my throat. "Tell me where you are."

"That's what I have been doing this whole time. But if you bring anyone with you, I'll slit your sister's throat before you ever get a chance to get her back."

"Wait," I say, rubbing my shaking palm over my face to clear my head. "Where? I don't understand."

"If you don't come for me, then I'll be coming for you."

The line goes dead and I drop my arm, slapping the phone against my thigh.

"Was it him? What did he say?" Dillon demands, his

palms on my shoulders, centering me. I wiggle from his grasp.

"Nothing that makes sense," I sigh, and then scream into the darkening sky.

"We'll get the call traced." He paces back and forth. "Did you know her?" he asks, pointing to the girl in the room.

"She's Bo's work colleague. The one he cheated on me with." I rub a hand through my hair.

"Do you know the reference to the creepy as fuck poem?"

I sigh and try not to think about my time locked away with him, but it's impossible and I'm launched back there before my next breath.

Benny hardly ever drinks, but when he does, it's always accompanied with the same solemn mood.

"Stand in the corner," he barks at me.

I do as I'm told and wait for him to enter. If he's under the influence, maybe I can get the upper hand and steal the key to my cell—wait for him to pass out and then free Macy and myself. The familiar clanking of the door didn't make me flinch as much anymore. You know you're fucked up when you get used to your abuse.

"Turn around."

I move to face him, not bothering to cover my modesty. He raped that from me a long time ago. Modesty is a joke.

"Whatever I say to you, I want you to repeat, 'I know, Benjamin'."

"Why?"

His jaw goes tense and ticks. "For one fucking day, can you just do as you're told?"

"I'm not a child, Benjamin," I huff.

Always the defiant one, I think it's what keeps me alive.

"If you don't do as I fucking ask, I will get my pretty little doll to do it instead," he growls, pointing a shaking finger past me.

Macy.

No.

"Okay, I'll say it."

"What are the words, dirty doll."

"I know, Benjamin," I stutter out.

His brows crush together and his chest rises and falls heavily. "Get on the bed on your stomach and spread those fucking legs wide for my cock."

I do as I'm told, swallowing the dryness in my throat. He's going to go in raw and it will hurt. Pain isn't a new thing for me, but I learned his moods and routines and could usually preempt his visits so I could prepare myself to accept him.

"Spread your fucking legs," he roars, and a tremor murmurs through me as I part my legs.

"Lift your ass and spread wider."

The bed isn't that wide and my knee shifts onto the metal frame as I push my ass into a prone position. His warm palm slides over my ass cheeks.

"I love this cunt, you know that? It's so fucking pretty. The pink is the perfect color for blush," he muses, leaning forward. His face smooshes against me as he inhales and then pulls away.

"I didn't get to taste her."

Her?

"But I bet she would smell and taste just as delectable as you do, dirty little doll."

I wait for his tongue to touch me there, but only cold air assaults me as his weight leaves the bed. "Don't move."

The clanking of my cell alerts me to him exiting and the door is left ajar. My head swims with thoughts of escape, but he's gone only a moment and I haven't moved. I would have never gotten to the door, let alone passed through it. I'm too busy thinking of my lack of escape to react when he snaps a handcuff around my wrist and to the bedpost. I wiggle my hand, but it's firm and I'm bound. Another clicking and cold metal snaps over my other wrist, attaching me to the other side.

"Ben..." I stop myself from finishing when his body stiffens next to me.

A cuff wraps around my ankle and then the bed, keeping me stuck in this position.

What's happening?

He repeats the process and my breathing increases in fear. The hiss and whip of the air as he extends a baton-looking object in his hand makes me flinch. His feet move to the bottom of the bed where I'm splayed open, vulnerable.

Miss Polly had a dolly who was sick, sick, sick.

Whack!

Pain like nothing before explodes against my exposed flesh.

So she phoned for the doctor to be quick, quick, quick.

Whack!

"P-please s-s-stop," I heave, gagging on the saliva filling

my mouth as tears I swore I'd never shed for him again pour from my eyes.

The doctor came with his bag and his hat,
Whack!
"Why? Please!"
And he knocked at the door with a rat-a-tat-tat.
Whack!
I'm going to pass out.
He looked at the dolly and he shook his head,
Whack!
The walls of my cell fade as the sound of his torture device hitting my most private place resonates in the small space.

And he said, "Miss Polly, put her straight to bed!"
Whack! *"You're dirty."*
He wrote on a paper for a pill, pill, pill,
Whack! *"You're dirty!" he screams, and as I drift into a state of unconsciousness, I think I hear him cry.*

"I'll be back in the morning, yes I will, will, will."
I wake to him on top of me. My limbs are free and I'm on my back, numb from the waist down to my knees. His heavy weight restricts my lungs from gaining air. Liquid drips onto my face and his tongue swipes it away.

"I'm so sorry," he coos. "She did this to us. We're not sick...you're not sick. Tell me," he urges, shaking my head with his giant palms grasping each side of my face.

"I know, Benjamin," I repeat, just like he instructed me to.

"I'm sorry. I love you."

"I know, Benjamin."

I gasp, catching the sorrow trying to escape my soul. He

hurt me so bad. Will I ever recover from this? The darkness steals me again and keeps me for days.

It took me forever to be able to move from that bed. I pissed it and every time I thought I was going to die from the agony, Benny would come into my cell and look at his work, telling me the bruising was a sign of healing. Then he would feed me water and it would send me back into the dreamless sleep. I give Benny one thing, he was so good at hurting me, making me bleed and bruise, swell and wish for death, but scarring me on the outside wasn't something he did. He liked me flawless for his sick perversion.

"Jade, you scared the shit out of me."

"Huh?"

"Where did you go, baby?" Dillon questions, pulling me into his arms. "You zoned out and couldn't hear me calling for you."

I gulp and swallow my fear. "He's never going to stop. He wants me back there." I break, my legs giving out. Dillon's arms tighten around me and he holds me to him. Then he swoops me off my feet and carries me like a husband would his new bride.

But there is nothing happy about this moment.

Fucking nothing.

I'm dying inside.

CHAPTER SEVENTEEN

~ Auburn ~

THE RIDE BACK TO MY place was silent. Since we arrived, he has undressed me, dutifully attempted to wash the horrors of the day from my body in the shower, and finally helped me climb into bed. Not a tear had fallen—no, I think I cried them all out already. The sting from the salty drops are still prominent on my cheeks, my eyes red and swollen from the fallen sorrow. The only thing I can feel now is anger.

White and blinding.

And it is building.

With each ragged and exhausted breath, molten fury rages hotter and hotter within me.

Dillon must be able to feel the heat. His fingers flutter over my warm naked flesh as if he's trying to calm the war waging inside me. I keep imagining my parents lying on slabs of cold metal, being cut into by the coroner. My mind races with their image and the thoughts that must have passed through their heads when Benny came for them…because of me.

Dirty little doll.

Why did I run? If I just stayed there, Bo would be living his life happy with someone who could give him more than I ever could. My folks wouldn't know what ever became of Macy and me, but they would still be alive. They wouldn't have had to die knowing what kind of monster still has their baby.

"Don't," Dillon breathes over me. "Don't blame yourself for any of this."

He kisses me on my lips, my face, my collarbone, and it drowns out the regret. His touch only adds fire to the already burning flames inside me. I want revenge. I want retribution. I want Macy back. The burning desire to fuck away the pain becomes so intense, I feel as though I may combust.

"Baby..." he murmurs, his mouth connecting with mine. "Listen to me." He's practically lying on top of me, crushing me with his weight.

I want him to smash me to smithereens, make me numb—steal away this explosive energy growing inside me. I'm going to self-destruct if he doesn't cling to me and ground me to him. Maybe if he crushes me to dust and consumes the ashes...

Maybe then I won't hurt so much inside.

Perhaps then, I'll feel empty.

His forehead presses against mine and his eyes look as though they are melted chocolate with the late afternoon sun peeking in through the window. "Baby..." he says again.

He probably wants to assure me everything will be okay. *Nothing will ever be okay.* He probably wants to tell me to sleep so I can dull the pain. *The pain will always be a sharp reminder of the monster in my life.* He'll probably beg me to seek counseling to find a way to deal with what

Benny has done to me. *I'll never find a way to deal until he's gone for good.*

"Baby," he says, his voice dipping low, "we're going to find him and we're going to fucking slaughter him. You and me, Jade. He's not going to get away with this. I'll be with you every step of the way and we will end him. Not by prison. He doesn't make it out of this alive."

It takes a moment to process his words. Of course Dillon wouldn't say what I expect him to. He's Dillon Scott. Arrogant cop with a sad past. A wild card in my predictable, hellish world. My insatiable lover with a passion for revenge. I should have known better.

"Thank you." My heart starts to throb back to life. Dillon makes me feel despite my yearning to never feel again.

He seems to know what I need because his lips crush against mine, painfully so. His kiss is deep and demanding—thorough and all-consuming. I hook my legs around his waist and urge him to me. That thick, hardened cock of his slides against my clit, weeping at the tip. I want him inside me so bad, I nearly choke out a sob, begging him.

"I know," he assures against my mouth. "I know what you need."

A long, drawn out moan rips from my chest as he eases his cock into me. I'm still getting used to his size. The way he seems to stretch me to capacity is dizzying.

"Fuck me hard, Dillon. Please, take it all away," I plead, the tears now streaming down my temples.

His Adam's apple bobs in his throat as he swallows and shakes his head. "I know what you need, and that ain't it, baby."

I start to protest, but he begins bucking into me. Slow, steady thrusts. His lips rain kisses down on my face, worshipping me with every peck. I claw at his shoulders, hoping he'll lose control like every other time and fuck me senseless. He doesn't. Those dark brown eyes remain fixated on mine as he makes love to me.

Sure, Bo made love to me plenty of times.

Hell, even Benny thought he did, the sick twisted fuck.

But they never made me feel so utterly consumed. Dillon's soul seems to reach into mine and cloak it with his protection and love. I feel safe—despite the tragedies I've faced today and in my past. Dillon finds a way to show me with his body that I'm not alone. That I'll never have to be alone again.

"My beautiful, broken girl," he murmurs against my mouth as he slides in and out of me in a torturous manner. "All of your pieces are mine to hold. Each shard is mine to willingly slice myself on. You're worth the pain. In fact, I want to embrace that pain if it means, even for one second, I can take some of that pain from you."

A sob escapes me and he kisses me softly. He rubs against me in such a way that my body begins to tingle and quiver with the need to release. This doesn't feel like a normal orgasm—it feels deeper and on a whole other level.

"I can't take the pain," I admit tearfully, choking on a sob. "It's too much, Dillon."

His forehead presses to mine again, his pace steady. "I know, baby. Give it to me. Just give it to me."

He kisses at the tears and over my closed lids, peppering me in delicate yet intense brushes of his lips.

The shudder that ripples within me is almost painful. Intense pleasure sears through me. I let it go. The pain that has a vise grip around my heart disappears for a moment as he groans out his own release. His heat soaks me from the inside and for one small second, I feel peace.

Dillon is peace.

I'm lost in this new world we've created—a world where nobody but us exists. There aren't psycho killers or dead family members. Just Dillon and I. Peaceful. He doesn't slip out of me as his cock softens. Instead, he slides his arms beneath me and hugs me to him, smashing me with his entire weight, lifting us so I'm straddling his lap. It's as though he's trying to mold our bodies into one. Our sweat soaked skin glistens under the moonlight seeping through the open blinds and he holds me while I shake.

He nuzzles my nose with his and then licks up my salty tears on my hot, swollen cheeks. It only makes me cry harder with him caring for me on such a basic level. Dillon just always seems to know what I need. Right now, he protects me and soothes me with his body. I thread my fingers into his hair, gripping him so he won't leave me.

"Don't leave me," I murmur. "You're the only thing I have left."

His cock hardens again and he begins moving inside me, guiding my hips with one strong hand on my waist. "Never, Jade."

"What if he finds a way to get what he wants? He's evaded us this long." The thought is one that will never go away.

He slides a hand to my jaw and grips it to the point of pain. Fire rages in his eyes and my heart pounds in response. His protectiveness ripples from him—scorching me. "I. Will. Never. Let. Him. Hurt. You. Again."

I sniffle and shake my head. "He always gets what he wants."

Dillon growls and bucks into me hard. I cry out as he thrusts like a madman, bringing my body down onto him as his hips spike up. His teeth clash with mine as he consumes me with a kiss I feel down to my marrow. My hands rake at the flesh on his back and his fingers bite into my hips, grinding me on him. His mouth devours my hard nipple as his thrusts cause my tits to bounce. Licking, sucking, tasting, consuming. Our pants create a soundtrack to our carnal escape. His cock pushes deeper than ever before and my walls cling to him, squeezing for release.

We're both swept up in this vortex of sexual bliss and connection until I'm crying out his name over and over again like some fucked up chant. He doesn't stop until he's unloaded more of his seed into me and this time when he stops, I'm no longer sobbing.

"I don't want him to win," I hiss out, gasping on the heated air.

His jaw clenches and eyes flicker with hate—mutual hate for the monster ruining my life. "Against us, baby," he tells me fiercely, "that motherfucker doesn't stand a goddamned chance."

"How you holdin' up, Phillips?" Chief Stanton questions, lines of worry crinkling his already aging face.

After Dillon fucked me until I was mentally numb,

he let us sleep and as soon as the sun kissed the bed sheet with its morning glow, he dragged me back up to the station because Chief wanted to see us.

I shrug my shoulders and sip the coffee we picked up at Starbucks on the way over here. "Hunky fucking dory, Chief," I deadpan.

Dillon boldly reaches over and takes my free hand. "She's dealing about as well as can be expected for someone who saw her parents' brutally murdered bodies. She's holding up and that's all anyone can expect. How do you think she's doing?"

Stanton glances at our hand holding, but nods. "I'm sorry. I just worry about you. When some psychopath targets one of our own, it gets everyone around here rattled. This fucker has evaded us long enough. We all want justice. Each of us wants to be the one to bring that prick in and throw him behind bars. It will happen, Phillips. We're working 'round the clock and checking every lead. He's not going to hurt you. That's a promise."

I swallow down my bitterness. "Benny's good. Always two steps ahead. He'll get what he wants." *Me.*

Chief shakes his head in denial. "No. Not this time. I've assigned a uniform to stay outside your place—always on duty. And from the looks of it," he says with an unamused raise of his eyebrow, "Dillon's taking good care of you. That psychopath isn't getting anywhere near you."

I don't even try to force a fake smile. Chief has no inclination of how determined Benny is. He'll stop at nothing. The asshole's made that perfectly clear.

"Any details on the phone?" Dillon questions.

Chief grumbles. "We couldn't trace his call, but we

did lift a partial print from the burner phone. Lab is running it through AFIS. Hopefully we'll get a hit. Let's all send a prayer to the man above that the prick is in the system."

Dillon squeezes my hand and a flutter of hope filters through me. For eight years, I've been chasing a ghost. Now, the ghost is very much alive and haunting the fuck out of me. But for the first time, we might be able to close in on him.

Hang in there, Macy.

Mom and Dad may be gone, but I'm still here.

"Scott," Chief huffs, "take Phillips, and for the love of God, make her eat something. Tomorrow, I'll brief you on any new details or if we get a hit on AFIS. Look after our girl."

"I want to work," I tell them both, and they just stare at me like I said I want to eat babies or some shit.

"Yeah, that's not going to happen, Phillips. You need to take time off and look after yourself. You have to bury your folks and grieve for your loss."

Bury them.

Oh God.

He gives me a curt nod before waving us out of the office. Dillon pulls me to my feet and wraps his arm over my shoulder as we exit. All eyes are on us as he parades me through the precinct, showing all of them I'm under his protection. We get a few raised eyebrows and crude remarks along the way, but I'm okay with that. I've never felt so accepted. The entire time I've worked here, I've been regarded as fragile and broken.

Dillon doesn't care about any of that and holds onto

me anyway.

It's us against them.

It's us against *him*.

"Are you going to stand there until I eat? Shouldn't you be off finding bad guys?" I snap. "Finding *our* bad guy?"

Dillon lifts a dark brow. "As a matter of fact, I'm not leaving this morning until you eat that waffle I made you. This past week, you've barely touched anything. If we're going to find him, I need you at full strength."

Dillon brought all the case files home with him and let me go through them while he works each day. My parents' file, he managed to keep away from me, and I was grateful to him for that. Seeing them in the flesh at their murder scene was bad enough. I couldn't handle their pictures. We had nothing. Benny is so clean, it's as if he's a genius when it comes to this sick shit. He isn't in the system and didn't leave DNA on the rape victim. He used and dumped Bo's vehicle, so we don't know what it is he drives himself. We have an image, but it's not the best resolution and could be anyone. I know for a fact Benny is isolated. He hardly ever left us alone, so he must not have friends or family. Posters and appeals went out this week with the image, but nothing that's led to anything substantial has come back.

"Jade?" Dillon queries at my silence.

With a curled lip of disgust, I stab at my waffle and make a great show of stuffing a piece into my mouth, even going as far as to chew with my mouth open. He chuckles, and for the first time in a week, I find myself fighting a genuine smile.

"You're a brat," he says, sipping his coffee.

"I just hate feeling like a prisoner."

He winces at my words and I instantly hate myself for even remotely comparing him to Benny. Benny held me against my will. Starved and tortured me. Raped me at every turn. His abuse was far from physical, though. He psychologically forced himself against me. Imbedded himself inside my brain and wreaked havoc. They are nothing alike.

"I'm sorry," I whisper, dropping my fork onto my plate. I stand from the chair and walk over to him. "I didn't mean it."

When I hug his middle, he sets his coffee down and hugs me back. "I know. You've been through a lot. Don't apologize to me."

This morning, after our long shower, he got dressed for work, but he smells too good. If I keep inhaling his chest, I might beg him to distract me some more—from the bed. He's really good at that.

"What if he gets me? I can't help but think he's waiting for us to slip up so he can swoop in and haul me back to that house. He's too quiet, Dillon. A week with no word," I say with a worried sigh.

On one hand, I'm glad my ghost is in hiding. Bodies aren't turning up all over the place. I was able to mourn my parents in some fucked up sense of peace…

I'll never fully be at peace, though. Not until he's gone.

But on the other hand, I'm worried about Bo. That his body is decomposing somewhere because Benny would never let him live. And what about Macy? What sort of

PRETTY STOLEN DOLLS

awful things is he making her witness? Do…

No.

The leads running dry are driving me just as crazy as when Benny was terrorizing my world at every turn just one short week ago. The partial print was inconclusive, the phone traces led nowhere, and there wasn't any forensic evidence that could help us. Each day, Dillon does what he can at the precinct and I scour the county land records for any clues to where that fucker is hiding with my sister and ex-boyfriend.

"He's not going to get you. Littleton stands guard out there all damn day and I'm here at night. Nobody's getting in here unless they go through one of us. You think anyone is going to take on Littleton? He was a linebacker in college. Kid's solid as fuck. You're safe, baby," Dillon says, kissing the top of my head.

I tilt my head to look up at him. He's so cute with his crooked grin and scruffy face. If my world weren't so fucked, we could truly be happy, I think. Dillon distracts me and makes me feel so alive, worthy and wanted—his.

My palms slide up his hard chest until I start tugging at the knot of his tie. He groans, but doesn't argue as I tear it away and then work at his buttons. When I reach the last one, he peels it from his body and lays it on the back of the chair. I bite on my bottom lip. He looks totally fuckable in his white undershirt practically painted on his sculpted flesh.

"I don't have to leave for another twenty minutes," he says with a growl before ripping his undershirt off. Every muscle on his chest flexes with his movement. "I can do a whole lot in twenty minutes, baby."

I smile and it reaches my eyes. God, he makes me happy despite this horrific shit happening all around me. "Can I keep you longer than twenty?"

He doesn't answer. Instead, he charges for me. Like the caveman he is, he tosses me over his shoulder, making me squeal with delight. His hand pops my ass through my panties and I smack at his ass since it's right in my face. When we reach my room, he tosses me onto the bed and wrangles out of his slacks and boxers while I peel off my shirt and panties in record speed.

"You're like a fucking drug, Jade. I can't seem to get you out of my system," he admits as he prowls on the bed toward me. "And I don't want to. I just want fucking more."

He jerks my knees apart roughly, and then he's inside me. Dillon hardly goes slow. That's one of the things I love about him. Most men would want to treat me delicately because of my past. Dillon just devours me.

And I want to be devoured by him.

"God!" I cry out as he slams into me. We haven't been together long, but our connection is intense and stronger than the one Bo and I had.

"So beautiful and broken and mine," he murmurs into my neck, his teeth nipping at the flesh. He knows my neck is my weak spot and seems to always drive me crazy there with his mouth.

"Yes," I hiss, "yours."

My fingernails rake down the front of his chest, causing him to hiss. When we fuck, neither of us leaves the bed without scratches, teeth marks, bruises, and sometimes the occasional blood.

Like I said.

He devours me.

And I devour him.

"Jade," he groans against my throat as we both come apart, a mutual shattering of worlds. "I-I-I," he grunts, "fuck, Jade."

"What?"

"I love being with you…this thing we have amongst all the chaos, it's real, right? You feel this growing between us?" He lifts up and stares down at me as if I'm some magical, spell-casting creature.

"I do," I assure him. I love this. Whatever it is we're doing, I love it.

"I'm so infected with this crazy lust and maddening lo—"

"Shhh. I feel it too. I'm yours," I assure him.

The pad of his thumb strokes under my eyes and then he drags it down along my nose as he regards me with wonder. I grip his wrist and frown. "Macy…" I murmur.

His dark brows furl together. "What about her?"

"She has a scar there. Along her nose. Benny cut her deep enough to scar her badly. If any bodies…if…" Tears well in my eyes and I blink them away. "I can't see her body too."

"Hey," he coos and cradles my face, pressing kisses all over me. "You won't have to see. Baby, we'll find her. She's his collateral—his only bargaining chip. We just have to find that house. We find his house, we find her. Then we'll bring her home to us."

To us.

I want to believe him.

So badly, I do.

I wake to the warm glow of the bathroom casting my bedroom in a dim light. Pushing the sheet from my body, I pad across the chilly floor, the scent from my shampoo washing over me as my hair sways around my shoulders.

Padding barefoot into the living room, I find Dillon still fully dressed and his hair standing up in tufts, like he's been there pulling at it. My stomach dips and I slowly approach him from behind.

I peek over his shoulder and see the file he's reading. It's the one from eight years ago, when I escaped Benny.

"Dillon."

He doesn't turn to look at me. His hands scrub down his face and he breathes in deep. "I knew, kinda. I didn't work the case, but we all heard about the girl who was kidnapped. How she was found alive, and even more remarkably, had escaped her captor. I knew…but I didn't fucking *know*, know." He pulls at his hair and I reach down and take his hands, sliding my body onto his lap.

He wraps his arms around my back and burrows his head into the nook between my shoulder and neck. His grip is almost painful, but I don't stop him. Hot mist blows over me from his heavy pants. "I hadn't read them. I couldn't. We have nothing else to go on, so I need to look for clues, but I…it's—fuck, Jade, what he did to you," he chokes, and I hold on to him.

I let him break.

For me.

For him.

For us.

"Isn't she pretty?" Benny questions. "Such a pretty little doll, like you."

I can hear him, but I've been blindfolded. He has me bound by my wrists above my head, but my legs are free. Unfortunately, he's also gagged me with a cloth so I can't speak.

I'd gone off on him earlier when he came into my cell. I'm starving and he left us without food or water for what felt like ages. When he returned and came into my cell, it was like the arguments Momma sometimes had with Daddy, accusing and hurtful.

I screamed that he couldn't do that, that he was a sick pervert and I hated him, and he froze, his whole body rigid. I affected him and I let the power of it explode.

"You're a disgusting pervert. No one could love an animal like you, Benny. *So whoever you've been off with for all this time is insane or fucking dead. Let's face it,* Benny, *you're ill. You have a sickness in you," I screamed, pummeling at his chest.*

He just let me. I built and built until he finally backhanded me across the face, and when I hit the floor from the impact, I lost consciousness. When I woke, this is how I was. The memory of the baton last time he cuffed me had terror engulfing me so strongly, my bladder released and I was now sitting in my own piss.

"What's that?" he bites out. And then a small squeak. "I asked you if she was pretty."

Macy.

"Y-Yes."

"Prettier than you, huh?"

A sniffle. "Yes."

"But she's so dirty too," he states, causing me to cringe.

"Very dirty," Macy agrees, her voice but a whisper.

"Shall I clean her up?"

Macy whimpers. "I want to go back to my bedroom."

Bedroom?

"Why, Dolly?" he asks, humor in his dark voice.

"Her room is dirty and scary."

"Do you hear that, dirty little doll?" he questions, his warm palm snaking up my naked thigh. "She doesn't like your room."

These are not rooms!

"Please, Benjamin," Macy pleads.

He chuckles. "Not just yet, Dolly. Tell your sister why your room is better."

Macy, with a hint of pride in her voice, explains, "The walls are pink, my favorite color. And there are so many beautiful dolls. I have a nice bedspread too."

Benny's thumb caresses the inside of my thigh. "That bedspread belonged to my sister, Bethany, but our mother never let her use it. Bethany was very pretty. Like Jade."

I freeze at his words.

"Am I pretty like them?" Macy questions, her voice sounding sad.

"No, Dolly. That scar is ugly. I'm sorry, but you're not like them. And that's your own fault, but you learned by your mistake. Your sister sadly refuses to, so she has to have many lessons and punishments." His reply is cold and empty.

She sniffles. "I think she's ugly right now. And dirty. She stinks." The contempt in her voice hurts my heart. Macy.

"Take it back," he chides, much like a father would his child.

"I'm sorry. I didn't mean it, Jade," she whimpers, and my heart cracks open.

"That's not her name!" he roars. "Sit over there in the corner, Dolly. You've both been naughty and should be punished."

I can hear her footsteps and then shuffling as she sits. She's whimpering, but he ignores her.

"Don't," I beg around the material filling my mouth, but he ignores my pleas.

"Dirty little doll," he says, his fingers creeping higher up my thigh. "That's her name. She's dirty. Aren't you?"

"No!" I scream into the gag and shake my head.

"Really? So, if I touch you here, where you are covered in your own fucking piss, will you not enjoy it?" His thumb presses against my clit and I jolt in shock. So often he's cruel, so the moments he's gentle, I don't know how to deal with him.

"Listen, Dolly," he clips as he massages me in a way that has me squirming. My body can't defend against his attacks when it's a reaction to an action. It's not lovers feeling pleasure; it's someone knowing how to make your own body—your own soul—betray you until you can't even stand to be you any longer. You'd rather be anyone else, and slowly, the you who lived in the carcass he abuses fades and becomes hollow.

"Listen to your sister, Dolly. She claims to hate me, but she lies. Her body shows me how much she loves me."

I hate you…I hate you…I hate you.

"Look how pretty she is right now." He pushes my legs

to part and when I try to close them, he pries them wider and digs his elbows into the soft flesh of my thighs. "She loves me. Look at her cunt twitching, begging me to love it."

Bile creeps up my throat and I almost force the sick to come up so I can choke to death on it behind the gag.

"Do you love me?" I hear Macy ask. My heart crumbles. This is how he reunites her with me? I can't see her, but she has to witness this?

"You want me to, don't you?" he says simply.

No!

My scream through the rag is muffled. Fat wet tears soak the blindfold.

"I do," Macy says softly.

No! No! No!

"One day, perhaps, if my dirty doll pushes me enough," Benny says, digging his fingers into my hips and causing a burning sting there. "But I'm not a pervert, pretty little doll, despite the lies your sister spilled earlier."

He digs harder and I wince, breathing deep to handle the pain.

"I like cleaning her up with my mouth. I get the best reactions from her."

And then his tongue replaces his thumb. His finger pushes inside me and I block it out for as long as possible until the nerve endings spark and my body deceives me. I'm so lost, drifting in confusion and trying to navigate away from the bliss my body seeks—teetering over the edge of sanity, overlooking the depths of the abyss of dark lunacy that's always lurking.

He sucks on my clit and I jolt. I can't hold off the sensations flooding my body and without permission, I fly over the edge. My cries become moans without consent. Benny becomes my pleasurer and not my torturer…even if only for a moment. And I hate him more than I ever had.

I'm getting out of here or I'll die trying.

CHAPTER EIGHTEEN

~ Rosso Corsa ~

"Wake up." Dillon's hot breath tickles my ear. "I have your dress ready."

I've been awake for a while, but haven't left the bed. Dillon carried me back here last night and we both just lay there and held each other in a firm, unbreakable embrace.

Going through the motions, I push back the sheet and make my way to the shower, ignoring the reflection screaming at me to get more sleep.

The hot spray rains over me and I wash my body and then step out into a towel Dillon is holding up for me. He pats over my skin, drying me, and then throws the towel to the bed. Picking up my clean panties he laid out, he taps one leg and then the other, dressing me like I'm a child. And I feel too numb to stop him. I lift my legs so he can roll the black pantyhose up my calves and then thighs. Lifting my arms, he slips my dress over and it falls around me, stopping just below the knee.

I force my feet into a pair of black ballet pumps and pull my hair back into a neat bun.

"You ready?"

I nod.

But I'll never be ready to bury my parents.

They died because of me.

―▶

Watching their matching caskets get lowered into the ground knowing the headstones they had chosen for Macy and I when they assumed we were dead will be put there for them when the ground has settled is a surreal moment.

Will I have to bury Macy next to them?

No.

Recognizing people surrounding their now gravesite but not actually knowing anyone anymore hurts deep inside my bones. I refused to go to the wake last night because of these people who are all now staring, wondering, accusing. I'm barely keeping it together around them.

"Can you take me to the bar for a drink before we go back home?" I ask, curling into Dillon's side. His arm wraps around me tight, keeping me standing.

"Don't you want to go to the reception, baby?"

"No." Shaking my head, I leave the warmth of his safety and move toward his car.

He doesn't speak the entire ride over to a bar near the precinct that is a favorite among my colleagues, but his hand holds mine firmly against his thigh. "You sure you can handle this lot?" He smirks, tilting his head toward Josie's Bar.

"Yeah, it will be a good distraction."

The voices boom and vibrate off the walls as the jukebox lulls in the background to their volume. Liquor and leather assault my senses, and I smile. I need this.

"Whiskey, straight up," I order, holding my fingers up to signal I want two.

"Hey, Phillips. Good to see you." Someone pats me on the back, but I don't see who. I down the whiskey as soon as the glass hits the coaster in front of me and tap it for a refill.

"Did someone die?" a voice jeers to the right of me.

"Her fucking parents, asshole," another says.

"Oh yeah, I forgot. Did they catch that guy yet or what?" He's drunk. I can tell from the slur in his tone.

"Shut the fuck up," Dillon barks over my head and moves to walk around me, but I place my hand on his tight, toned stomach, willing him to take a seat.

"Simmons, that's enough," someone else grunts.

Simmons was my old partner. He tried to get frisky with me once and I hit him right on his nose, nearly breaking it. Apparently, he's still bitter.

"Has anyone questioned her? Let's face it. We all know she's fucking crazy," Simmons says with an obnoxious laugh. "I say she tipped over the edge and went on a rampage," he bellows, and my insides churn as the white hot anger returns in full force. I stand to stop Dillon as he darts from his stool. Turning, I force my palm up and connect with Simmons' nose. It's fast, hard, and effective. Blood sprays everyone standing too close and his feet stumble backwards. Grabbing the pint on the bar, I tip it over his head and smash the glass at his feet.

"Sober up, asshole. You're embarrassing yourself."

"You stupid cunt," he roars. "You really fucking broke it this time!" A fist hitting flesh signals Dillon laying him clean out and everyone rushes to carry him out of the bar.

"No one thinks that, Phillips," Marcus chimes.

It doesn't matter what anyone thinks. I know the

truth.

Dirty little doll.

Fresh air blasts over me as we exit the bar and I turn to smile at Dillon. "My hero," I say with a smirk, pulling my dress up my thighs and leaping into his arms.

"He's had a thing for you for years. I don't know where that came from," he growls, pacing with me attached to him.

"It felt good breaking his nose for real this time." I smile against his lips, feeling a little lighter. Maybe violence is what I needed to get out some of this pent up anger inside me.

I grind my pussy against his cock and he hisses.

"Fuck me in your car, Dillon," I moan, biting his lip.

"People will see," he groans against my attack.

"Let them see," I tell him and then giggle.

Explaining the emotions swirling and twisting inside my head right now would be impossible. There's this insurmountable amount of agony eating at me but also this intense passion anchoring me, like a black hole trying to swallow a star but coming up against immense gravity stopping it from going under. Dillon is the gravity and he's keeping me from being devoured.

Opening the car door, he drops me to my feet and clambers inside, undoing his zipper and releasing his sizable cock. He waves his hands at me, gesturing for me to climb on and I have to bite my lip to stop from laughing at his enthusiasm. Reaching for the hem of my dress, I lift it and point to my pantyhose. Launching forward, he grabs me toward him and I have to place my hands on the roof to stop from falling into the car. His strong grip grabs me between the legs and tugs. The ripping sound excites me and my panties dampen.

"Now, get in here," he orders playfully.

I slip over his lap, my back to his front, and he gasps at my position.

Hovering over him, I hold the dash while he yanks my dress higher and scoots my panties to the side. His fingers test my opening, pushing inside my walls and pumping hard.

"You're all wet, baby. And look at this ass all in my fucking face. I want to eat it."

He lines his cock up and lowers me on to it. My thighs are pressed together, causing my entrance to be tighter as I lower onto him. His cock stretches and fills me, and we both gasp and pant as my pussy strangles his full length. I use the dash to push my weight back on him and his hips wiggle and writhe beneath me as his strong hands rotate and grind my hips down. "You're so fucking tight."

Moving his hands up, he roughly cups my tits and pulls me back against him so he can kiss and lap at my earlobe and down my neck. One hand snakes down and finds my clit, swollen and throbbing. He spanks it and then squeezes until I come undone, screaming his name for all to hear.

My heart pounds and my pussy contracts, milking him for his climax. We topple over together and it's a state of bliss I've never reached before.

Peace.

CHAPTER NINETEEN

~ *Electric Crimson* ~

"I'M SO GLAD YOU DECIDED to come back."

I give her the once over and hold back my cringe. The shoes she has on don't match the crimson of her skirt.

I love that color.

"My parents died." I speak into the room and she visibly startles. I count the fish as I make my way over to them. One, two, three, four, five, six, seven, eight, nine.

"Parents. As in both?"

Was I speaking another language? How does this woman even call herself a doctor?

"Yes, both," I snap, impatience lacing my tone. "They were murdered."

"Oh my God," she chokes. "I'm so sorry. Do you want to sit?"

I shake my head no and gaze once more at her fish. All nine of them. This will be the last visit I make here.

"Do they know who murdered them?" she queries, shock still evident in her tone. It's higher and breathier than usual.

"I think so. Maybe." I shrug. Tapping my finger on the tank, I look over my shoulder at her. "Did you know fish will eat a human body?" I ask, turning back to the pointless creatures. I sense her shift in her seat without having to look at her. "They will see it as any other food, strip it of its nutrients, and poop out the rest," I laugh without humor.

"That's off topic," she says with a weary sigh. "Why don't you come and have a seat?"

I look over at her once more and she's scratching at a small scar on her hand.

"It's a phantom itch."

Her brow furrows and her head tilts like a puppy, not understanding the superior being in the room.

"The nerve endings are dead in scars," I tell the stupid woman. "The need to scratch is a phantom itch."

"Oh." She quickly covers her scar and shakes her head. "I'm not sure if that's correct."

Marching over to where she's sitting, I lean into her, causing her to rear back and point my finger in my face. "Look," I bite out, spittle showering over her eyes, cheeks, and nose, "I know about scars, lady."

The scar Benjamin gave me sometimes itches, but it's in my mind. He tells me so.

Fear swirls in her eyes, but I'm so bored by her. What a sad life she leads here in this open spaced coffin.

"I want you to have some comfort," I tell her. It's a lie, though. I just like taunting her. It's the best part.

"I don't understand. Macy, can you please take your seat?" Her voice shakes.

"That's the problem," I seethe. "You really don't understand and that makes you a real shitty doctor. My name isn't Macy. It's Pretty Little Doll."

"That's not a name." Tears well in her eyes.

How dare she tell me my given name by my master isn't my real name.

"Just know," I hiss as I pull the blade from the pocket of my beautiful dress. "Your head will feed your fish for a while."

Her eyes enlarge at my words and her body begins to react, but it's too slow. My blade comes across her throat like a hot spoon through ice cream. I bite my lip and lean further into her so she can be in this moment with me. I watch confusion, fear, sorrow, and lastly, acceptance flash in her dull eyes.

Her body lifts and gasps against mine and I embrace the moment she gives in—the moment her body stops beneath mine. Her head flops back, causing the spray to pump out faster, covering me in a shower of her blood.

Benjamin will punish me for ruining my dress.

Time passes quickly as I busy myself with my task.

Eventually, the door opens and closes behind me with a click. It's been over an hour and he promised he would be back in an hour. I pull away from her so I can regard him. His gaze skims over the mess I've made. I've just finished separating the good doctor's head from her shoulders and it hangs by her hair in my fist.

It's really hard cutting through bone. Luckily, she has a kitchen fully stocked with carving knifes.

With a pretty smile I know he likes, I prance over to the tank and drop the head in with a splash. The crimson flow from her neck colors the water in seconds.

"Look at the state of you." Benjamin's cold tone drenches me with shame.

"I'm sorry," I mutter, bending down and swiping my fingertips through the blood. With a hasty swipe, I smear it across my bottom lip.

"Cerise, your favorite," I offer, willing him to come to me.

He doesn't.

He never does.

"It's time, pretty little doll," he tells me, his voice softer this time. "Go wash up."

CHAPTER TWENTY

~ *Blood* ~

MY SLEEP IS DISTURBED—ONE NIGHTMARE bleeds into the next. I can't get comfortable and keep fading in and out, confused by what's real and what isn't. Stanton called and said Adam Maine, the hit-and-run vic, awoke in the hospital and his recount is crucial to the investigation. Dillon didn't let me go with him, though. Apparently it might spook the vic. He didn't deserve what he got, but it's still irritating calling him a victim.

The bed dips next to me and warmth floods through me.

Dillon.

My eyelids flutter open and pretty hazel eyes stare back at me. So often when I awake from nightmarish memories, she lingers. My sweet, little sister lingers for a moment and I desperately hold on to her.

Her dark hair is in cute plaits like I remember doing for her when we were little, to keep the heat at bay. The scar is silvery, but still very prominent. Those pouty lips that match mine are painted bright pink. My eyes drop to her pretty dress that matches her lip color.

She always seems so real.

Macy.

Reaching forward, I finger a strand of her hair. Her hazel eyes flicker with emotion, but she doesn't disintegrate into the air. Not this time—not yet.

I must still be asleep. This has to be a dream.

"Macy," I breathe, her scent, flowery and pungent, filling my nostrils

Thud.

Thud.

Thud.

This time, I'm able to hold onto her for a moment longer. She so vivid.

"Macy," I murmur.

Thud.

She reaches up for my hand, blood caked on her creamy flesh.

Thud.

The familiar stirrings of my memories collide with my nightmares. In my nightmares, she's always hurt and bleeding.

"I'm so sorry I left you."

In every dream, it's always the same. I tell her what I can't physically say.

"Shhh," she whispers. "It will all be over soon."

"I killed our parents," I sob. "They're dead because of me."

Thud.

"Daddy was so consumed with teaching us about monsters," she murmurs. "He never saw when they were right in front of him." She reaches for me, and I reach for her too. I think she might take my hand, but she places something into my palm instead. It's cold and gooey.

Thud.

My eyes lower and a scream lodges in my throat.

My father's eyes.

No.

Thud.

"It's okay, dirty little doll. It will all be over soon."

No.

Her hand lifts once more and she brings a white, lacey handkerchief to my face stained with the blood from her hand. A whiff of something chemical invades my senses—not at all what I was expecting—and then everything fades back to nothingness.

CHAPTER TWENTY-ONE

~ *Lust* ~

Dillon

Leaving Jade at the apartment, knowing she's going out of her mind, is getting harder with each new day. We have nothing. Zero. Fucking zilch. This Adam Maine is our last hope for a lead. Anything he can tell us could give us something to run with.

We need to find this sonofabitch, get him off the street, and finally give Jade some peace.

My girl hates Benny…Benjamin—whatever he wants to call himself. To me, he's the sick fuck, and I harbor a unique detestation for him that is all mine to keep. When I finally get my hands on this motherfucker, I will extract payment in blood and flesh. He is coming apart, piece by disgusting piece.

I flash my badge to the guard at the door of Adam Maine's hospital room and go inside. He looks like shit. Tubes attached to monitors beeping around him and nearly every fucking inch of him in a cast.

"He can only talk in small amounts and we can give you two minutes' maximum," a plump nurse with age lines showing signs of a hard life tells me.

I'll make every minute count.

"I'm detective Scott." I flash him my badge. "Do you remember where you were held before you were brought into the hospital?"

"No." His word is but a hissed, painful whisper.

"Can you tell me if the man mentioned a location or why he held you before bringing you to the hospital?"

His brow furrows and he winces. "No, man."

"No, man?"

"Woman," he clarifies, his voice shaky.

"Oh, I know a woman brought you in." I nod. "I'm talking about the man who hit you."

"Woman," he states again, anxiety in his voice.

"We know you weren't attacked by the police woman, Adam, so you can drop the act." Irritation courses through me.

"A. Woman. Hit. Me," he blasts in spluttered breaths.

"A woman was driving the truck?"

"Yes." His eyes close and then slowly open.

"Was she the one who held you captive until you were brought here?"

"Yes. I. Tackled. Her. But. She's. Fucking. Crazy."

I dart from the room to the security area on floor four. The door opens on my approach and a guy I recognize as Buddy stands there. I've worked with him on occasion over the years. He must have seen me on the monitors.

"Hey, man, what's up?"

"I need you to bring up the footage of Adam Maine being brought in. Look on your computer at his admitted time stamp and bring up the material from that day," I bark.

He senses my tense, don't-fuck-with-me attitude and does as I ask.

My heart is going to burst out of my chest and flip around on the floor.

Fuck.

Fuck.

Fuck.

Buddy taps over keys and brings up different monitors, and then it's there—a woman who looks like my girl. Her face lifts up to the camera.

"Freeze the image," I order. "Zoom in."

He does as I ask and my hand shakes as I reach for my cell. I swipe at the screen with the other hand as I wait for the ringing tone to sound in my ear. My fingers slide down the scar on the girl's face.

Macy Phillips.

"Answer, baby."

"This is Detective Phillips. I can't take your call right now. Leave a message and I'll get back to you."

I run from the room and down the corridor, shouting for people to move out of my way. "Baby, please be sleeping, or showering, or God—anything," I whisper to myself. "I love you. I love you, Jade. I'm coming home."

I make it to my car in a blur and begin driving. My head is swimming. This will break her.

Littleton isn't there when I pull up and my fear ricochets through every nerve ending, landing in my heart with a sickening *thud*.

No.

No way.

No fucking way.

She's going to be up there asleep. He took a piss break—he has to piss at some point.

My feet carry me at a speed I didn't know I was capable of to her apartment. The door stands ajar.

Fuck.

Fuck.

Fuck.

No.

Pushing the door open, I jerk my gun from its holster and creep through her apartment. All the things I left unsaid to her plow into my mind like a nuke going off inside me, obliterating my soul. She doesn't know I love her. I didn't say the actual full words. She doesn't know.

And I lied.

I didn't protect her.

I let him get to her.

I let *them* get to her.

I reach her bedroom and acid surges through my blood and settles in the marrow of my bones.

A disturbed bed sheet sits crumbled on the floor and there's blood.

Fuck.

Screams buzz from the corridor and I don't want to go see why. Tears burn in my eyes for the first time since Laney died. My chest is tight and compressing in on itself. I'm moving toward the commotion. A woman is screaming at the door of another apartment. She's pointing with one hand while holding the other to her mouth.

"She's dead."

My feet move in slow motion.

Thud. Stomp. Thud. Stomp. Thud. Stomp.

Entering the apartment, air I was holding in my lungs leaves my body in a hiss.

It's not her.

It's not fucking her.

Thank fucking God.

"Oh sweet Jesus, someone killed my therapist," the woman sobs.

And although it's fucking horrid seeing a woman's head floating in a fish tank, I know it's not my girl. Not my broken, lost girl.

They fucking have her.

And I'm going to get her back.

·

CHAPTER TWENTY-TWO

~ Fire Brick ~

Jade

My nostrils sting and my body aches. Sensitive and bruised.

I roll my neck and force my heavy lids to open. It takes a couple tries, but they open and burn as they do. My sight is blurry as my retinas adjust to the light. The memories of my dream rush to the forefront of my mind and I quickly raise my hand. There's blood there.

Thud.

I sit up and my head swims. I'm woozy. The walls around me come into focus and my lungs seize. Air hisses from me when my eyes dip to see I'm naked.

No.

Thud.

Clank!

I jump from the tiny bed of the cell from so many years ago.

No.

The door slams shut and the lock kicks into place.

No.

Thud.

Thud.

Dark, haunting pits of hell look in at me. And the ice-cold voice that could freeze the sun fills my ears from the little bars separating us.

"Welcome home, dirty little doll."

The End…for now!

Find out what happens in the epic, thrilling conclusion coming soon called
Pretty Lost Dolls

Benny had a dolly who was sick, sick, sick.
Just like him, his dolly needed darkness as a fix, fix, fix.
So they tormented and hunted and played tricks, tricks, tricks.
Together their sins a lethal mix, mix, mix.

Until Benny missed his dolly who was lost, lost, lost.
He needed to find her and love her at any cost, cost, cost.
Not wanting him and his dolly to be alone, lone, lone.
He made plans to bring his dirty dolly, home, home, home.

Have you ever touched another's soul with the essence of your own, breathed them in so they become apart of you?
I have.
Finally starting to live, feel and fall in love, amongst all the chaos surrounding me.
Dropping my guard and letting another into my heart.
I left my soul open.
I left my heart open.
I left the door open.
And he stole me.
Dillon…I'm sorry.

PLAYLIST

Listen on Spotify

Stand By Me – Ki: Theory
The Devil Within – Digital Daggers
Doll Parts – Hole
Run, Run, Run – Tokio Hotel
Mad World (feat. Gary Jules) – Michael Andrews
Sweet Dreams – Marilyn Manson
Psycho Killer – Talking Heads
Where Is My Mind? – Pixies
Tainted Love – Marilyn Manson
You're So Vain – Marilyn Manson
To Be Alone – Hozier
Where Did You Sleep Last Night – Nirvana
All The Pretty Girls – Kaleo

ACKNOWLEDGMENTS FROM
Ker Dukey

Thank you to K Webster for being patient and risking shoulder paralysis to get the cover perfect. It's been a pleasure to explore and share her mind as we constructed these characters and brought them to life on the pages. Huge thank you to my amazing PA, Terrie, who sorts all the packets and reveals ect…ect.

My street team, who share and spread the word. To Webster's girls who share this task.
Word Nerd Editing, Monica, thank you for your love this book and your awesomeness giving it the finishing touches.

Champagne Formats, Stacey, never fails me. I ADORE YOU.

And last but in no means least, to YOU! The reader. Thank you for sharing this journey with me/us and for your passion, you blow me/us away.

BOOKS BY KER DUKEY

THE DECEPTION SERIES
FaCade
Cadence
Beneath Innocence - Novella

MEN IN NUMBERS
Ten
Six

EMPATHY SERIES
Empathy
Desolate

THE BROKEN SERIES
The Broken
The Broken Parts Of Us
The Broken Tethers That Bind Us – Novella
The Forever Broken – A Broken Novella – coming soon

A STANDALONE NOVEL:
My Soul Keeper

THE BAD BLOOD SERIES
The Beats In Rift
The fire In Ice –TBA-

Lost – A stand alone novel

ACKNOWLEDGEMENTS FROM
K Webster

A huge thank you to Ker Dukey for reaching out to me to ask if I wanted to take a walk on the dark side with you. It was a pleasure skipping through our wicked world laughing maniacally all the way. Writing with you was a joy and I look forward to writing more twistedness with you! You're a star!

Thank you to my husband, Matt. You're always there to love and support me. I can't thank you enough. I'll be your pretty little doll until the end of time…and sometimes I'll even be your *dirty* little doll.

A huge thanks to Elizabeth Clinton and Ella Stewart. Thank you always being so supportive and quick to read my stuff no matter what. You are great friends!

Thank you to Sunny Borek…you always support my dark adventures and love my bad guys!

Thanks to Nikki McCrae. I appreciate all you do for me!

I want to thank the people who either beta read this book or proofed it early. You all gave me great feedback and the support I needed to carry on. You all give me helpful ideas to make my stories better and give me incredible encouragement. I appreciate all of your comments and suggestions.

Also, I want to thank Vanessa Renee Place for dropping everything to read this book and watch for any last minute mistakes. Thank you!

A big thank you to my author friends who have given me your friendship and your support. You have no idea how much that means to me.

Thank you to all of my blogger friends both big and small that go above and beyond to always share my stuff. You all rock! #AllBlogsMatter

I'm especially thankful for my Krazy for K Webster's Books reader group. You ladies are wonderful with your support and friendship. Each and every single one of you is amazingly supportive and caring. I love that we can all be weird page sniffers together.

I am totally thankful for my author group, the COPA gals, for being there when I need to take a load off and whine. Y'all rock!

A huge thanks to Monica with Word Nerd Editing for taking care of our precious dolly book and making it as perfect as it could be!

Thank you Stacey Blake for making this book GORGEOUS like always! Love you!
A huge thank you to Terrie Arasin for taking me under

your wing and help me navigate the promo of this book without thinking I'm too much of a spaz!

A big thanks to my PR gal, Nicole Blanchard. You are fabulous at what you do and keep me on track! Also a big thanks to the ladies over at The Hype PR!

Lastly but certainly not least of all, thank you to all of the wonderful readers out there that are willing to hear my stories and enjoy my characters like I do. It means the world to me!

BOOKS BY K WEBSTER

THE BREAKING THE RULES SERIES:
Broken (Book 1)
Wrong (Book 2)
Scarred (Book 3)
Mistake (Book 4)
Crushed (Book 5 – a novella)

THE VEGAS ACES SERIES:
Rock Country (Book 1)
Rock Heart (Book 2)
Rock Bottom (Book 3)

THE BECOMING HER SERIES:
Becoming Lady Thomas (Book 1)
Becoming Countess Dumont (Book 2)
Becoming Mrs. Benedict (Book 3)

Alpha & Omega
Omega & Love

WAR & PEACE DUET
This is War, Baby
This is Love, Baby
This Isn't Over, Baby

STANDALONE NOVELS
Apartment 2B
Love and Law
Moth to a Flame
Erased
The Road Back to Us
Give Me Yesterday
Running Free
Dirty Ugly Toy (Dark Romance)
Zeke's Eden
Sweet Jayne
Untimely You

Printed in Great Britain
by Amazon